THE PRICE OF PARADISE

DEFIANCE #5

JASON KRUMBINE

Published by Lantern Key Books

ISBN: 978-1-971197-04-3

Originally published in 2020 by Jason Krumbine

First Lantern Key Books Edition: December 2025

about this book

When Nax left his home planet he had no intention of ever returning and he certainly didn't anticipate being dragged back to face charges of High Treason.

Under Natuzzi law, the charge of High Treason carries only one possible punishment: Death.

While the Natuzzi are considered a valued member of the United Planetary Alliance, they are also considered to be notoriously xenophobic. They prefer to keep non-Natuzzis off their planet and out of their affairs.

Under the guise of maintaining diplomatic relations, Nax is abandoned by the UPA Fleet Admiralty. As far as they are concerned, if Nax has broken Natuzzi law, then the Natuzzi can have their pound of flesh and any attempt made to interfere with the Natuzzi legal process would be considered an act of war.

Captain Gavin Mitchell, however, doesn't see it that way. He'll do whatever it takes to protect a member of his crew. Even if it means starting a war that no one will win.

Books in the Defiance Series

Defiance
Hand of God
Act of God
The Test of Truth
The Price of Paradise
The Value of Terror
The Last Breath of a Dying Tomorrow

Subscribe to my newsletter and I'll let you know as soon as the next Defiance book is ready to read.

https://onestrayword.beehiiv.com/subscribe

THE PRICE OF PARADISE

previously...

The USS Defiance has been docked at Starbase Atlantic for much needed repairs.

While docked there, the UPA's ambassador to the Veneer is murdered by Joseph Michael Cavige.

Joseph Michael Cavige is the head of a religious organization known as the Church of Eternal Clarity.

The Church of Eternal Clarity is a cult-like church that actively engages in brainwashing, blackmailing, exploitive practices and physical and emotional abuse. All of these charges and accusations are currently unfounded as the church has yet to be found guilty of anything. Despite all this, the Church of Eternal Clarity is considered one of the most popular religions in the Alliance and enjoys having the ear of the current political administration that is governing the United Planetary Alliance.

The Church of Eternal Clarity is extremely litigious and is actively preparing to fight the charges against Joseph Michael Cavige.

Viv'an Bendare is one of the richest citizens in the UPA. She is worth nearly six billion credits. Her primary business is as a black-market arms dealer, but she has found success among other criminal activities. Due to her relationship with Ambassador Reynoso she chose to provide assistance to the UPA legal team, albeit without them knowing, and intercepted the Church of Eternal Clarity long enough for Cavige to be arrested and charged.

Recently it was discovered that Lt. Commander Nax is actually a member of the Natuzzi Royal Family and is wanted for High Treason against the Natuzzi people.

1

NATUZZI

"HAVE you anything to say for yourself?" the woman asked.

Lt. Commander Nax did not answer.

He stood in the center of the large room, his hands restrained in front of him. A harsh spotlight, projected from the stone ceiling, shone down on him, casting a bright glow around him that extended nearly two feet in every direction.

"Nothing at all?" she asked.

The woman, like Nax, like all Natuzzi, had orange skin and was completely hairless. Her bald head was slightly narrower and, from afar, in the darkness of the tribunal room, one would be forgiven for mistaking her age. Like most Natuzzi, she had aged gracefully. Her orange skin had yet to show the telltale signs of darkening and wrinkles that most Natuzzi gain at this point in their lives. It was her eyes, though, that gave her away. They were sharp, focused, and cast an intimidating gaze. But there was no mistaking the years behind those eyes.

When Nax refused to answer, she sighed, a sound that echoed softly in the chamber, and folded her hands upon the curved desk. The flowing sleeves of her robes collapsed gently across the surface. She looked to either side, as if silently asking the other members of the tribunal, 'What am I to do with this troublesome child?'

Two guards stood directly behind Nax, on either side of the main doors. They were dressed in the armored uniforms of the Royal Guardsmen. Their weapons were holstered, but there was no way, if he had been inclined, for Nax to make it to the exit in time. The Royal Guardsmen were the most elite and lethal of the Natuzzi military. Despite their relaxed posture, either one of them would be able to pull their weapon and deliver a kill shot before Nax ever moved out of the spotlight.

At the table, on either side of the woman, sat four other members of the tribunal. They were all women and were all dressed in the same white robes. The only difference between the other four members and the woman Nax refused to answer, was the crown that sat upon her head.

"Very well," the Queen said after a silence that had threatened to go on forever. "You stand before this tribunal accused of multiple crimes: abandonment and dereliction of duties, unauthorized travel off-planet, and worst of all, carnal relations with a non-Natuzzi."

The last charge seemed to suck the air out of the room. The other four members of the tribunal were visibly disgusted. But it was the guards who truly couldn't contain themselves and one of them audibly gasped.

The Queen glanced disapprovingly at the guard and he immediately lowered his gaze.

"Apologies, Your Majesty," the guard said hastily.

She flicked her tongue against her teeth loudly. "There are going to be details revealed here that will be scandalous. They will be unseemly, and unsavory. You will hear of actions that are unbecoming of a member of the royal house. There will be testimony that you will undoubtedly find to be heart-wrenchingly disturbing." She paused to take a breath, casting her gaze back to Nax. "It will be uncomfortable to hear all this. But you will maintain your sense of order and decorum as you do. If you do not, there will be *consequences*." She looked back at the guards. "Do we have an understanding?"

"Yes, Your Majesty," both guards said in unison.

"Good." She turned back to Nax. "Prince Kinlin Nax, do you dispute these charges?"

For a moment, Nax said nothing

Beside him, Grace Hawkins appeared. As always, she was dressed in her Fleet uniform. Her dark hair hung loosely around her shoulders. Nax took great care not to look in her direction. She didn't say anything and for that, he was grateful.

Then she reached out, her fingers caressing the back of his hand.

Nax flinched slightly at her touch.

The Queen noted this, but did not speak to it.

No one else in the tribunal room, of course, could see Grace Hawkins. She was there only for Nax.

"I dispute nothing," Nax said. His voice sounded briefly strained.

Hawkins nodded, as if he was speaking to her, and then took a step back, disappearing to wherever she disappeared to when she wasn't with him.

This time it was the other members of the tribunal who could not contain themselves. They muttered in disbelief.

Instead of delivering another unnecessary lecture, the woman rapped her knuckles sharply against the surface of the table and the tribunal fell silent.

"Of course you don't." The woman brushed back the sleeves of her robes. "Very well. How then do you plead?"

With Grace gone, Nax found himself relaxing again. He rolled his shoulders back and raised a hairless eyebrow. "How do I plead?"

"Did I misspeak?"

"I was under the impression that it doesn't matter how I plead, as you have already found me guilty."

"Indeed we have."

"So it really doesn't matter how I plead, then," Nax replied.

For a moment, she didn't speak. She simply stared at him, her lips quivering slightly with visibly restrained rage. Slowly, and with great care, she pointed a long, narrow finger at him. "You have broken our most *sacred* of laws."

Nax shrugged. "Well, in my defense, you weren't supposed to ever find out."

She gaped at him in shock. "*That's* your defense?"

"I thought about putting something together that was a little more complex, but it all boiled down to the same basic argument: You weren't supposed to find out."

The woman scowled. "Do you think this is a joke?"

"Has the punishment for high treason changed since I left?" Nax asked.

"It has not."

"Then, no. I definitely do not think this is a joke."

She leaned forward, her face a mask of anger and confusion. "You never intended to return home?" It was a statement disguised as a question.

"Is that something I need to actually answer?" Nax asked. "Because it seems fairly self-evident that I clearly did not."

"You are a traitor to your people."

"As you've already said," Nax replied, unfazed.

"Perhaps you don't think this is a joke, but you are certainly not treating it with the seriousness that it deserves."

"Would you prefer that I grovel for my life?"

She scowled at him again. "I could have you executed on this very spot."

Nax nodded. "And I would expect nothing less of you, Mother."

2

USS DEFIANCE

JUST OUTSIDE OF NATUZZI SPACE

"YOU WANT to run that by me one more time?" Captain Gavin Mitchell asked. He glared at the man on the monitor. "There must be some kind of interference because it sounded like you just told me that we're going to leave a member of my crew to the mercy of some kangaroo court."

The man on the monitor was Admiral Stewart Perlman. "Mitchell, don't you start with me," he growled.

"I just had a member of my crew forcibly removed from my ship," Mitchell said. "I already started."

"Did they hold you at gun point?" Perlman asked. "Did they have their weapons trained on the *Defiance* and threaten to blow you out of the sector if you didn't hand over Nax?"

"No," Mitchell growled.

"You're damn right they didn't," Perlman said. "Nax turned himself in under his own volition. So why don't you take it down a few notches."

Mitchell took a deep breath and unclenched his fist. "Lt. Commander Nax is not only a member of my crew, but he's also a citizen of the UPA. Last time I checked, he's supposed to be afforded certain inalienable rights, which include not getting tried for treason on some trumped-up charges."

"Trumped up charges?" Perlman echoed.

"Have you seen the charges?"

"No."

"Neither have I."

"Doesn't make them any less valid."

"That's not how this works," Mitchell said.

"The Natuzzi government submitted their case to Fleet Legal and they determined it is how it works," Perlman said. "They want to charge Nax with treason, they're well within their rights to do so."

"And that's it?"

"Is there something else you were expecting?"

"Who's defending him?"

"Do I look like I've got an inside track on the Natuzzi legal system, Mitchell?"

"No, but you look like a man who's too damn quick to sell out one of his own."

"One of our own?" Perlman shook his head. "Have you taken a look at Commander Nax's file lately? Nothing in it even hints at his status as Natuzzi royalty. That's a hell of a thing to leave out. Tell me, Mitchell, were you aware of Mr. Nax's status as royalty?"

"I was not," Mitchell replied.

"How are you feeling about that?"

"Since when is privacy a crime?" Mitchell asked.

"When it's an attempt to cover up past crimes," Perlman replied.

"And what were those crimes again?"

"Treason."

"And what does the Natuzzi government consider to be treasonous behavior?" Mitchell asked.

Perlman didn't respond.

"And what's the punishment for treason under the current Natuzzi government?"

Perlman didn't have an answer for that either.

Mitchell nodded. "That's right. We don't know because the Natuzzi don't permit outsiders access to any of their planetary databases. So, for all we know Nax's act of treason could be having stolen a piece of bread from the wrong table and he's going to be executed for it."

"I highly doubt that the Natuzzi still implement the death penalty for anything," Perlman said.

"Considering how little they share with the rest of the Alliance, I don't."

"You got a point to make, Captain?"

"I'm pretty sure I'm making it, Admiral."

"What the hell do you want to do, Mitchell? Storm in there with guns a-blazing?"

"It's not Plan A," Mitchell replied. "But it's on the list."

Perlman nodded. "Sure. That sounds like a reasonable response. Let's go pick a fight with a UPA planet. I'm sure that'll go over real well with literally everyone."

"They started it," Mitchell said.

"This isn't some schoolyard tussle, Mitchell," Perlman snapped. "I'm not letting you get us into a conflict with an ally over one of their citizens who's been lying to us for the last decade."

"Lt. Commander Nax is not only an officer in good standing with the Fleet, but he's a good man and an upstanding citizen of the UPA."

"Well, according to the Natuzzi he's a member of the ruling family who disappeared a little over ten years ago," Perlman said. "Presumably because he was evading charges of treason."

"I don't believe it."

"I don't remember asking if you did," Perlman said.

"And what about you, Admiral? Is this what you believe?"

"I believe that despite whatever good Mr. Nax has done since joining the Fleet, it's not enough to erase any crimes he might have committed in the past."

"And that's it?"

"Pretty much."

"So we're just going to leave him there?"

"As a matter of fact, that's exactly what we're going to do," Perlman said.

"He deserves better than that."

"I don't entirely disagree," Perlman admitted. "But until the Natuzzi suggest otherwise, Mr. Nax is no longer our problem."

"He's still a member of my crew," Mitchell said. "His problems are my problems."

Perlman frowned. "Let me be perfectly clear, Captain Mitchell: No one is happy about this. It's bad all around and there's nothing you can do that's going to make it any better. Do you understand?"

"Yes, I do, Admiral."

"You know what? I don't think I'm making myself clear enough." He jabbed a finger at Mitchell. "Consider this a *direct order*: You are *not* to enter Natuzzi space without direct clearance from *me* personally. Do you understand *that*?"

"Perfectly," Mitchell replied coldly.

Perlman glared at him. "Don't screw around with this, Mitchell. This is the only warning you're going to get."

3

"Well, it's official," Mitchell said, addressing the group at the conference table. "Mr. Nax is on his own."

"What the hell is that supposed to mean?" Rabkin grumbled.

"It means that the Fleet is washing their hands of him," Mitchell said.

"That's a hell of a raw deal," Rabkin said. "What's their logic for that?"

Mitchell gripped the back of his chair tightly. "He lied about his status as a member of the Royal Family, therefore we don't know what else he may have been lying about."

"Bullshit," Rabkin said.

"Preaching to the choir, old man."

"Tell us the UPA's at least sending a legal representative on his behalf," Sadler said. She sat next to Rabkin.

"They're not," Mitchell said.

"That makes sense," Warrick said. He and Keane sat across from Rabkin and Sadler. "The Natuzzi don't like letting in off-worlders for even basic commerce. You better believe they sure as hell won't let us in on any legal proceedings."

"Bullshit," Rabkin repeated. "What are our orders?"

"Our orders." Mitchell took a deep breath as he sat down. "Our orders are to not do a damn thing. We're not to cross over into Natuzzi space. We're not to attempt any contact with Nax. In fact, Admiral Perlman would like it if we got back on our scheduled assignment seeing as how our ship is space worthy again."

"Bullshit," Rabkin said.

"Amen to that," Keane said.

"What are we going to do?" Rabkin asked.

Mitchell didn't say anything for a moment. He just stared at the surface of the table, drumming his fingers to a random beat. Eventually, he looked up at Warrick. "How much did you know?"

"Captain?"

"Mr. Nax is a member of the Natuzzi Royal Family," Mitchell said. "And that's just the tip of the iceberg. How much of this iceberg did you already know about?"

The Chief Engineer didn't answer right away. He ran his hands across his bald head and leaned back in his chair. "Pretty much all of it," he admitted.

"Swell," Mitchell said. "How come this is the first I'm hearing about it?"

"It wasn't something Nax wanted anyone to know," Warrick said.

"And how do you think that's working out for him?" Mitchell asked.

"Captain," Warrick started.

Mitchell shook his head. "I'm not interested in excuses, Warrick."

"I'm not offering any," Warrick said. "Just wasn't my place to go around blabbing his personal details."

"What did he do?" Mitchell asked.

"Do?" Warrick echoed.

"Why are they charging him with treason?"

Warrick shrugged. "I have no idea."

"That's not going to be very helpful."

"It's the truth, though, Capt'n," Warrick said. "Hell, they didn't even know he left the planet in the first place."

Mitchell raised an eyebrow, but didn't say anything.

Warrick sighed and shook his head. "Well, they weren't supposed to know."

"Every time I think this is going to start making sense, it gets even more confusing," Mitchell said.

Warrick took a breath. "Captain, you have to understand, Nax is a very private individual."

"So I'm learning."

"The things I know, they were not entrusted to me lightly."

Mitchell folded his arms and leaned back in his seat. "Mr. Warrick, you've spent some time on Natuzzi. In fact, as I understand it, you're one of five humans who's actually set foot on the planet and only the third who's spent any considerable amount of time there. This is, of course, assuming that your Fleet record isn't filled with a bunch of grade school creative writing assignments, either."

Warrick held up a finger. "Nothing in Nax's file is a lie."

"A lie of omission is still a lie, Mr. Warrick."

"If he had listed his status as a member of the Royal Family, he would have never been accepted into the Fleet," Warrick said.

"And we wouldn't be in this particular situation right now," Mitchell said.

"There'd also be a lot of people who'd be dead if Nax hadn't been in Directive Fifty-Two," Warrick said.

Mitchell frowned. "Somehow I feel like you think I'm interested in playing a game here."

Warrick sighed. "I don't think that at all, sir."

"Then instead of playing 'What If' why don't you start answering my questions."

Warrick shifted in his seat. "I was on Natuzzi for nearly six years."

Keane whistled under his breath. "How the hell did you pull that off?"

"It's...complicated," Warrick said. "The whole thing involved two life debts and I ended up overstaying my welcome by about four years. My last two years on the planet, I was essentially a wanted man."

"Wonderful," Mitchell said. "Is there a warrant out for your arrest, too?"

"Only if I set foot back on the planet," Warrick said. "Otherwise, they don't really care."

Mitchell pinched the bridge of his nose and closed his eyes for a second. "Unbelievable," he muttered.

"Could be worse," Rabkin said.

Mitchell opened his eyes and looked at the doctor. "Exactly how could this be worse?"

Rabkin shrugged. "How the hell should I know? Do I look like a damn psychic? All I know is that it could be worse. Shit can always get worse."

Mitchell shook his head and turned back to Warrick. "Are we going to have a secondary Natuzzi problem with you, Mr. Warrick?"

"As long as I stay off the planet and word doesn't get back that I've been blabbering all the Natuzzi secrets that I promised not to share, we should be just fine."

"What other secrets are you sitting on?" Mitchell asked.

"All due respect, Captain, I'd rather not say," Warrick replied. "I think we should keep this on a need-to-know basis."

"A need-to-know basis?" Mitchell echoed.

"I took my vows very seriously."

"I'm sure you did," Mitchell said. "Tell me, Warrick, what's the punishment for treason on Natuzzi?"

Warrick hesitated. "It's death."

"Shit," Sadler muttered.

Mitchell nodded. "So I think it's safe to say that we probably need to know everything. We can weed out the garbage as we go."

Warrick sighed. "Nax may be a member of the Royal Family, but he's not exactly a vital member. He's the first-born of Queen Xie, but he's not even in line for the throne."

"I'm pretty sure that's not how that works," Sadler said. "I read a lot of historical dramas and the firstborn is literally always the first in line for the throne."

"Not on Natuzzi," Warrick said. He paused and took a deep breath. "Because they're a matriarchy. There's your first big secret."

"The Natuzzi ambassador to the UPA is a man," Keane said. It was an awkward statement and even he realized it almost immediately. Keane shook his head. "I mean, there's no record of this. There's plenty of interactions with Natuzzi superiors and they've all been men."

"They're a matriarchy, not monsters. It's not like they're going to keep their men locked up in the dungeons. There's plenty of work for Natuzzi men," Warrick said. "They can hold positions of power, but every one of them answers to a woman. There's not a single department, organization, political office, or military assignment that's not headed up by a woman. And at the top of that food chain, is Queen Xie, Nax's mother. So thanks to his gentlemanly man parts, he's not eligible for the throne.

"When I met him, Nax wasn't exactly on speaking terms with the rest of his family. I don't know what the specifics were and he never cared enough to tell me and I never felt like pushing the issue. I only knew of his mother through the Natuzzi newsfeeds and she seemed like a real piece of work." Warrick shrugged. "I didn't think there was much of a mystery to the family drama. Nax lived on the southern peninsula in a small fishing village and didn't have much in the way of responsibilities. When he decided to leave, he figured the odds were pretty good they wouldn't notice for a while, if ever. Near as we could tell, it seemed like nobody from the Royal Family even knew he was in this village in the first place."

"Why'd he feel like he had to sneak off?" Keane asked. "Royalty, even royalty that's not in line for a throne, should still have the freedom to leave the planet whenever they feel like it."

"Except that Natuzzi aren't allowed to leave their planet without a departure visa," Warrick said. "In order to get a departure visa, you have to apply for one. Their State Department only hands out about thirty every solar cycle, and that's for the entire planet. Every Natuzzi that goes off-planet is accounted for. The government likes to keep tabs on the whereabouts of every one of their citizens. There are no exceptions. Not even for members of the royal elite."

"Nax is a member of the Fleet," Sadler said. "How the hell did he get that far without anyone back on Natuzzi realizing where he was?"

"Hell, the man's a Directive Fifty-Two operative," Keane

said. "How the hell does this not show up on his background check?"

"We forged his documents," Warrick admitted.

"Of course you did," Mitchell said.

"And that didn't come up on Directive Fifty-Two's radar?" Keane asked.

"I know a guy who's really good at it," Warrick said. "For starters, Nax's identification number belongs to a Natuzzi who was given clearance to join the Fleet a few years back, but he died before signing up," Warrick explained. "Took some creative paperwork, but that's basically how Nax's been off-planet for the last fifteen years."

Mitchell rubbed his face. "I really don't want to know any of this."

Warrick shrugged. "You asked."

"And I'm regretting having asked. So what are the consequences for leaving Natuzzi without permission?" Mitchell asked.

"In most cases, jail time," Warrick said. "In a handful of cases where the individual had a little more power and resources available to them than the average Natuzzi, there's a fine instead."

"How'd they find him?" Keane asked. "That's a hell of a long time to go without being found."

Rabkin grunted. "I think that's my fault."

Warrick turned to him in surprise. "Say what now?"

Rabkin folded his hands on the table. "When Nax was struggling with his bout of insomnia, I hit a wall, because, hey, nobody's had the opportunity to examine a Natuzzi like this before and I had no idea what the hell I was looking at. So, I reached out to the Natuzzi government, requesting his medical records and any other cases that might be similar to his. They politely told me to fuck off and that was the end of it."

"Son of a bitch," Warrick muttered. "Your request must have set off an alert on somebody's desk: why the hell was a Fleet doctor inquiring about the medical records of a member of the Royal Family? When they went to go ask Nax about it, they realized he wasn't around to ask."

"Whoops," Rabkin said.

"Great," Mitchell said. "So that mystery is solved. Now maybe somebody can tell me what the hell he was running from?"

"I wouldn't say he was running," Warrick said.

"What you described is literally the definition of a man on the run," Keane said.

"Because of societal conditions," Warrick said. "Not because he did anything to run from."

"Are you sure about that?" Mitchell asked.

"One hundred percent certain, Captain," Warrick said, meeting Mitchell's gaze. "Nax wasn't running from anything."

"He's been charged with High Treason against the Natuzzi people," Mitchell said. "If they're not going to execute him for running out on his duties as a member of the Royal Family, then what the hell would they execute him for?"

Warrick took a deep breath and exhaled slowly. "Falling in love with Grace Hawkins."

4

NATUZZI

It didn't look like a prison, but it certainly felt like one.

Nax looked around the room, expecting something different. But it hadn't changed since the last time he had been here. Of all the things he had been prepared for, being locked in his childhood bedroom hadn't been one of them.

"It's nice," Hawkins said, leaning back on the bed, her hands propped up behind her. "I always wondered what you were like as a child." Her gaze lingered over the sterile nature of the room. "And this doesn't do anything to answer that question. Seriously." She sat up, folding her arms. "This place looks like a grandmother's bedroom. *This* was your childhood room?"

Nax didn't respond. He rubbed his wrists. The restraints had been removed, but he still felt their echo. He walked around the room slowly, looking for something that was out of place. He may be the son of the Queen and this may be his childhood bedroom, but he was still an enemy of the state.

"The room's not bugged," Hawkins said.

Nax stopped in front of the wardrobe that was made

from the silver bark of the dustvelour tree. There were intricate swirls carved into its surface, creating a dizzying effect that had so delighted him as a child. It used to be twice his size. Now it felt small and unimpressive. He glanced over his shoulder at Hawkins, who was still sitting on the bed.

"Oh, come on," she said. "Like I don't know what you're thinking."

Nax didn't say anything.

"You don't have to say anything," she said and tapped the side of her head. "After all, I'm in here with you. We're beyond words now."

Nax turned back to the wardrobe and opened it. It was empty. He wasn't sure what expected. It would have been ridiculous to find his clothes still hanging inside.

"But everything else is the same around here," Hawkins said.

"Stop it," he said under his breath.

"The room isn't bugged," she repeated. "Nobody's listening."

He closed the wardrobe and moved over to the window.

"Of course, I'm sure somebody's watching that window," Hawkins said. "So if you bother to talk to me from there, you'll probably have an awkward conversation with somebody where you'll have to explain who you were talking to."

Nax turned his back to the window and faced her.

Hawkins smiled and crossed her legs. "Did I say something wrong?"

"How do you know the room isn't bugged?"

"Because you know it isn't bugged. Your mother may be many things, but you know she's not the type to bug your childhood bedroom."

"She could have put me in the dungeon," he said.

"Is that supposed to be an argument in her favor?" Hawkins

asked. "Because I don't see how that's relevant. Sounds like you're just spouting off random facts about your mother."

"She could have put me in the dungeon," Nax said again. "Instead she put me here: my childhood bedroom."

"Ah." Hawkins nodded. "You think there must be an ulterior motive."

"It stands to reason."

"Well, I can't argue with that. After all, she's your mother. It's not like I got a chance to meet her." Hawkins paused, thinking it over. "Do you think she would have liked me? I mean, ignoring the part where I'm not Natuzzi, because obviously your mother and the rest of your people are xenophobic assholes. But outside of that, do I seem like the kind of person your mother would have liked?"

"She wouldn't have liked Grace."

"*I'm* Grace."

Nax narrowed his gaze. "You are not Grace Hawkins."

She tilted her head to the side. "Are you sure about that."

"Yes."

"Well, you haven't exactly been forthcoming about your identity either." Hawkins wagged a finger at him.

"Is that a confession?"

"No. It's me pointing out that people who live in glass houses shouldn't throw stones."

"I never lied about who I was."

"No, but you also conveniently never mentioned you were *royalty*." Hawkins gasped theatrically. "You have to admit, that's a hell of a thing to leave out."

Nax crossed the room, looking for a seat that wasn't on the bed. "I was going to tell you."

"Were you? Really? Because I think we both know that's bullshit."

He stopped in the middle of the room and looked back at her. "How come you didn't know?"

"Because out all of the things I could have guessed you were hiding from me, being a member of the Royal Family didn't even make the top ten."

"I meant *now*."

"Because I don't see any reason not to respect your privacy," she replied.

Nax grunted. "Interesting."

"Interesting? How so?"

"You don't have access to my mind," Nax said. "Or, at least you don't have access to all of it."

Hawkins took a breath and exhaled slowly through her nose. "So you're really doubling down on this?"

"It's the only thing that makes sense?"

"Are you sure about that?"

Nax hesitated. "Yes."

"*Please.*" Hawkins rolled her eyes and got to her feet. "So if I'm not a product of your diseased mind, what am I? A ghost?"

"You're not Grace."

"Why would I be a ghost of somebody else who's pretending to look like your dead lover?"

"I don't know," he replied. "I've never had the opportunity to speak with a ghost before, so I'm not familiar with the motivations of the departed."

"You don't think I'm a ghost, though."

"I think you're certainly something different."

She walked up to him and placed a hand on his chest. "If I'm not Grace, then who am I?"

"I don't know," Nax said. "And to be honest, it's a mystery I don't have the time to deal with right now as my focus needs to be on ensuring that my mother doesn't execute me."

"She wouldn't kick a man while he's down, would she?" Hawkins asked. "After all, it just seems like cruel and unusual punishment to execute a man suffering from Fey's Euphoria."

Nax's breath caught for a moment and he brushed her hand from him. "I'm not willing to make that play."

"Are you sure? The pity play can go a long way," Hawkins said. "Especially with moms. Besides, it would conveniently hand wave away all of the charges. You weren't in your right mind. Poof, problem solved. Sure, that means you'll have to live out the rest of your days with a stigma of Fey's, but at least you're alive."

"That would mean I wasn't in my right mind when I met you."

Hawkins shrugged. "It would keep you alive."

"By sacrificing what we had."

"In fairness, I'm already dead, so it's not like you're sacrificing all that much."

"It would be a cut too far," Nax said.

"Don't be dramatic."

"I loved her too much to forsake her like that."

Hawkins raised her eyes. "*Her*? We're talking about *me*."

"You're not her."

"I might as well be."

Nax looked her over slowly, before settling his gaze back on hers. "I will accept no substitutes."

She smiled again and raised a hand to caress the side of his face. "That's not what you said the other night."

He caught her hand before she could touch him. She flinched slightly at his grip, but the playfulness never left her face. "Oh, is there another side of you I'm going to meet now?"

"Stop it," he said.

Hawkins moved in closer, pressing her body against his. "I don't think you want me to."

Nax tightened his grip on her wrist. "You are not real."

She glanced at her wrist in his hand. "I certainly feel real, don't I?" Her hand groped him between the legs.

Nax let out a startled gasp.

"You know, I never thought about the possibility of doing it in your childhood bedroom," Hawkins said. "But now that's all I can think about."

"Stop," he hissed.

Her grin turned wicked as she squeezed him. "What's the matter? Are you afraid your mother's going to walk in on us?"

Nax abruptly let go of her and jerked back out of her reach. He wiped his hand down the side of his uniform. "You're not Grace," he said again. His voice was shaky this time.

"Are you sure about that?" she asked again.

This time he didn't answer.

"Okay then." She clasped her hands behind her back and spun around on her heels. "When you die, what do you think is going to happen to me?" She glanced back at him when he didn't answer. "Do I die? Do I die again? Or is it the first time for me?"

Nax stared at her wordlessly.

"Maybe we can haunt each other?" she suggested. "That would certainly be a change of pace, wouldn't it?" She grinned again. "Or maybe we could haunt somebody together? Your mother?" She made a face and shook her head. "Ew. Never mind. I don't know why I suggested that."

Nax turned to face the door, his hands clenched into fists.

Hawkins sighed. "It doesn't have to be like this," she said. "You can ignore me. But that doesn't mean I'll go away. I mean, I haven't yet. So, I don't know why you think this'll be any different."

Nax didn't say anything. He just stared at the door and waited.

5

USS DEFIANCE

"This is the big one," Warrick said. "This is the one law that the Natuzzi won't mess around with. It supersedes all other laws. Basically, you don't fuck with off-worlders." He winced. "I'm paraphrasing."

"Are you sure about that?" Rabkin asked. "That sounds like some pretty official language there."

"The Natuzzi are all about keeping their bloodlines pure," Warrick explained. "That means nobody has sex with a non-Natuzzi."

"I hate to be the one that has to mention this," Rabkin said dryly. "But not all sex ends in procreation."

Warrick shook his head. "Doesn't matter. Because every time two people have sex, there's a chance at procreation and no matter how slim that chance, it's too big for the Natuzzi."

Sadler rubbed her face tiredly. "I don't understand. Why is this such a thing?"

"Well, it goes right to the core tenets of the Natuzzi philosophy, which is, essentially, anybody that's not Natuzzi doesn't count. And if a Natuzzi and say, a human can have sex and produce a baby, that means either: A, humans *count*, they co-exist with Natuzzi as a viable species in the universe and that invalidates the uniqueness of the Natuzzi. Or B, it means that the Natuzzi don't *count*, they're as invalid as the rest of the galaxy and therefore they have no purpose."

"Well, shit," Rabkin muttered.

"Yeah," Warrick said. "It's...not a good look. But it's basically the one rule that the rest of their society is built around. Why do they keep off-worlders off planet? To limit the possibility of intimate contacts. Why do they limit Natuzzi from leaving the planet? To limit the possibility of intimate contacts. Why do they refuse most imports and exports? To limit the possibility of intimate contacts. You getting the picture here? If they discovered Nax had a relationship with Commander Hawkins, then yes, as far as Natuzzi law is considered, he committed treason of the highest order."

"But Hawkins is dead," Keane said. "Not only that, it's not like they had a kid."

"Doesn't matter," Warrick said. "He still broke the law. And yes, they could execute him for that."

"But will they?" Mitchell asked."

Warrick held up his hands. "Honestly? I have no idea. At the end of the day, he's still the Queen's son. Maybe she wants to make an example of him, or she decides to play favorites. It could go either way. Or..."

"Or what?" Mitchell asked when Warrick didn't continue.

Warrick scratched the back of his head and stared down at the table. He opened his mouth and then closed it.

"Mr. Warrick, don't make me ask you again," Mitchell said.

"There's one more possibility," Warrick said. "But to be

honest with you, Captain, I don't really feel like it's my place to share it."

"Well, unfortunately, Mr. Nax isn't here right now," Mitchell said.

Warrick sighed and pressed his hands against the edge of the table. "This is something that the Natuzzi *really* don't want out there. The fact that I even know about it is, well, *problematic* at best. And the only reason I know is because I basically swore a blood oath to never speak about it. If the Natuzzi government knew that I knew, I probably wouldn't have left the planet alive."

Mitchell twirled an impatient finger. "Enough with the preamble, Mr. Warrick."

Warrick took a deep breath. "There's this...disease. It's called Fey's Euphoria."

"As far as diseases go, that one doesn't sound too bad," Sadler said.

"Wait for it," Warrick said. "It affects, oh, they estimate about forty percent of the Natuzzi male population."

Rabkin raised his bushy eyebrows. "Only the men?"

"Official numbers say that it's present in less than five percent of the female population," Warrick said.

"Interesting numbers," Rabkin said.

Warrick tilted his head to the side and nodded. "Well, I wouldn't be surprised if they're being fudged a little."

"What's the disease?" Keane asked.

"It's degenerative," Warrick said.

Rabkin leaned forward suddenly, cutting Warrick off. "It affects a Natuzzi's perception of what's real and what isn't."

Warrick blinked, looking at him in surprise. "How the hell do you know that?"

"There's been rumors about this for years," Rabkin said. "Nothing specific and nothing easily proven. And certainly none of them suggested that it's as widespread as you just said. But a few years back I heard some doctors in the Alliance Medical Corps talking about something awfully similar. It was a thirdhand account to them, so I figured it wasn't exactly reliable. But a little later I heard something similar from an Aurrod doctor based out of one of the quasidium mining colonies on the far side of the Stroiter system. There's a handful of Natuzzi expats spread out there. Never even crossed my mind when I was examining Nax, though."

"Which is kind of the point," Warrick said. "The Natuzzi really don't want this information out there. Can you imagine what the fallout would be if the Alliance were to find out that nearly half of the Natuzzi population suffers from waking hallucinations?"

"The UPA would issue health sanctions against them," Keane said. "All trade would get shutdown until it could be determined whether or not the disease was contagious."

Warrick nodded. "But the real hit would be to their reputation: How is the rest of the galaxy supposed to take them seriously if we think they're seeing space unicorns everywhere?"

"Does Nax have this disease?" Mitchell asked.

"To be honest, I have no idea," Warrick admitted.

"Then what the hell is the point of all this?" Mitchell asked.

"Shortly after Hawkins died, Nax said he started seeing her," Warrick paused, but nobody said anything "He saw her and he would talk to her and she would talk back."

"Sure sounds like Fey's Euphoria to me," Rabkin said.

"That's what I thought," Warrick agreed.

"But you don't think that now?" Sadler asked.

"I don't know what to think," Warrick said. "I met several Natuzzi men that were afflicted with Fey's and Nax doesn't behave like any of them. He *knows* that he's talking to a figment of his imagination. Which means, by that definition, he's not really suffering from Fey's."

"Sounds like a case of semantics," Mitchell said.

Warrick shrugged. "Maybe. But I'm not a doctor."

Mitchell looked at Rabkin.

The old man shook his head. "Don't look at me. I don't have any special insight here. Best I got to go on are some half-baked rumors shared over a couple shots of Kusalax ale."

Mitchell turned back to Warrick. "How does this play with the charges of treason?"

"Typically the Natuzzi treat those afflicted with Fey's a lot like most other cultures treat basic handicaps," Warrick said. "A lot of these people are basically placed in long-term care facilities or, if their families are able to, they take on the responsibility of care for the victims a lot like you would take in an aging family member. The Natuzzi need to keep the profile low on Fey's, so they make sure there aren't any waves to upset anybody afflicted with it or anyone related to somebody who's afflicted with it."

"So if Nax is diagnosed with Fey's, they're not going to want to execute him since it might lead to a higher profile on the disease," Mitchell said.

"Of course, if Nax isn't diagnosed, none of that matters," Rabkin pointed out.

"But the Natuzzi government doesn't know what kind of extensive examinations you've done on Nax," Warrick pointed out. "There might be a concern that you've stumbled across something that could point to Fey's at a later date."

"I'm flattered they think so highly of my diagnostic skills," Rabkin said.

"So, wait, how does this help us?" Sadler asked. "Does this mean there's a possibility we can get Nax out of there?"

"Absolutely not," Warrick said.

"What?"

"Don't get me wrong," Warrick said. "He's my best friend and I would literally do *anything* for him. But the Natuzzi are never going to let him leave that planet. *Ever.* If they did-"

"It would basically validate everything that Nax has already done," Mitchell finished for him. "It would validate the existential existence of anything or anyone that isn't Natuzzi."

Warrick nodded. "Exactly."

A somber silence fell on the table.

Sadler looked around the room. "So what the hell are we supposed to do?"

6

NATUZZI

"Do you have a plan?"

Nax lay on the bed, staring up at the ceiling of his childhood bedroom. Beside him Hawkins was on her side, her head propped up under her elbow.

When he didn't answer, she poked at him. "Hey, I'm talking to you."

Nax folded his hands atop his abdomen and didn't say anything.

"This isn't going to make for fun times if you're not going to talk to me."

"Good," he replied.

Hawkins frowned. "That seems harsh."

Nax shrugged.

She sat up, sitting crisscross on the bed. "What exactly changed here? At what point did I become an undesirable?"

He slowly turned his head to face her. "When it became apparent that you aren't who you say you are."

She wagged her finger at him. "Except, you don't really believe that."

"I'm not sure what I believe anymore."

"Exactly."

He turned back to the ceiling.

Hawkins sighed. "Are you just going to lie here and wait for the guards to come back?"

"It seems as good a plan as any."

"And what if they come back to take you to your own execution?"

"Then obviously I won't be bothered with the mystery of you anymore," he replied.

Hawkins leaned forward until her face filled his line of sight. "Am I really that much of a bother?"

Nax frowned. "Perhaps it would help if you examined it from my point of view."

"Well, being visited by my recently deceased love sounds pretty swell to me."

"Even if you were simply a ghost, how would your haunting me help me move on?"

She shrugged. "Maybe I don't want you to move on."

"Exactly."

Hawkins sighed. "Come on."

He rolled away from her and sat up, swinging his legs over the edge of the bed. "At some point I will need to let go of your memory."

"That sounds terrible."

"It certainly does," he agreed. "But eventually it won't feel that way."

"That sounds even worse."

"Maybe. But I think that's how grief is supposed to work. I'm not supposed to live with it indefinitely."

"So, what? I'm supposed to just drift off into the ether and get completely forgotten?"

"Not completely."

"You'll forgive me if I don't find that particularly reassuring."

"In fairness," he said, glancing back at her. "If you're truly dead, your feelings aren't really that relevant to me."

Hawkins frowned. "You think if you're mean to me I'll go away?"

"The thought occurred to me," he admitted.

"Did you realize how stupid it sounded right away or did it take a few seconds?"

"The alternative," he said, ignoring her question, "is that, of course, you're not really Grace. And if you're not really Grace, then what are you?"

"A figment of your diseased mind," she said. "We covered this already."

"That's certainly a possibility," he admitted. "But not a likely one."

"Because I know something about some obscure Natuzzi figure that you don't know? It's possible you read about Bon Dov and simply forgot that you read about him."

"It's possible, but not likely."

"It's also possible that I made up the person," she said.

"And if you're a figment of my diseased mind, I then have to wonder why my mind would be playing tricks like that on me."

"It's diseased," she said. "You're not well. You're hallucinating your dead lover. That sounds like a pretty solid explanation to me."

"There is a third possibility," Nax said, getting to his feet. "You're something else."

She raised an eyebrow. "Something else?"

"Something foreign."

"You think I'm some alien entity that's taken up residence inside your head?" She chuckled. "Which seems more likely to you: you're losing your mind or you've been infected by an alien host?"

Nax didn't have an answer to that.

She hopped off the bed. "I don't know why you want to make this difficult."

"It's already difficult," Nax said. "I'm being haunted by my dead lover."

"It's not like I'm not being discreet," she said.

"Discretion is not the answer I'm looking for."

"It may be the only answer you get."

"Then perhaps my life has reached its natural conclusion."

"That's...dark," Hawkins said. "A minute ago you were trying to make sure you *didn't* get executed."

"I'm not certain I want to spend the rest of my natural life being haunted by you," Nax said. "And if that's what's in store for me, then my execution would be the most ideal next step."

She walked over to him, her hands extended to embrace him.

Nax stepped back as she drew closer.

Hawkins stopped and let her arms drop to her sides. "You don't mean that."

"You're the one inside my head," Nax said. "I think you know otherwise."

"Is it really that bad?" she asked.

"It's certainly not ideal."

"And is that enough to want to be *dead*?"

"No other solution seems to be presenting itself right now."

"You mean no other solution that involves getting rid of *me*." She pointed to her chest. "Because I can think of *plenty* of solutions that involve the two of us happily co-existing for a very long time in a mutually fulfilling relationship."

"I cannot imagine any long-term scenario where this could be happy for either one of us," Nax replied.

"It's been working so far," Hawkins said, there was a tremble in her voice, as if she was on the verge of tears.

"Simply because it hasn't imploded yet isn't proof that it's not going to."

She stared at him, not saying anything for a moment. "That's cold, even for you."

"Perhaps," he admitted. "But even in the best-case scenario, you're not real and I'm only being mean to myself."

"And if I really am Grace?" she asked. "If I really am her? Here, right now? Speaking to you?" She held out her hands. "Reaching out to you? Then what?"

"Then existence itself is far crueler than I ever imagined."

There was a sharp knock at the door.

Hawkins gasped quietly at the sound.

Nax turned, trying to keep an eye on her and address the visitor at the door, but before he could say anything, the door opened.

A tall, striking woman swept into the room.

Out of the corner of his eye, Nax noticed that Hawkins was no longer there.

He turned and gave his full attention to his new guest.

"Mother."

7

"It is good to see you again."

Nax raised a dubious eyebrow at this.

Queen Xie settled herself into the chair opposite his bed. Nax stood at the window, his back to her, unable to face her.

She gave a heavy, irritated sigh. "It would be nice to see more than just your back, however."

Nax's shoulders bunched up and he hesitated before turning around. It had been a long time since he had been alone with his mother. A very long time.

Slowly, Nax turned around and was surprised by two things.

One, Grace was nowhere to be seen. He nearly breathed a sigh of relief, but caught himself at the last second.

The second thing was how his mother didn't look any different.

In the tribunal room, it had been too easy to lose the notion of his mother to the trappings of the office and the pageantry of the situation. Here though, in his childhood bedroom, stripped away from all that, he was instantly struck by the fact that his mother didn't look any different than she had when he had left for that village on the southern peninsula.

She sat in the chair, looking neither relaxed or uncomfortable. She simply sat there, her back straight, her legs crossed and her hands resting on the armrests of the chair. Her orange skin was a little lighter than he remembered. There were a few wrinkles along her face. Undoubtedly there were other differences, other changes, but it was as though Nax's mind refused to acknowledge them. It locked down on the aspects of her that remained close enough to his last memory of her and seemed to insist that the rest of her remained unchanged.

The crown that had adorned her head was gone. It was an uncomfortable piece of ceremonial jewelry that she wore only in public. Within the privacy of the palace, Queen Xie was simply dressed in a white, billowy outfit that managed to look regal and casual all at once.

She looked him over. "Well?"

Her voice sounded older, he realized. In the tribunal room, where she had used a more regal, authoritative tone, he hadn't noticed it. Here, though, in his childhood bedroom, he became all too aware of the slight quiver of age in her voice.

"Is there something specific you're expecting me to say?" Nax asked, clasping his hands behind his back.

"You could start with showing some gratitude." She gestured to the room. "I could have tossed you into the dungeon."

"You could have had me executed on the spot in the tribunal room," Nax reminded her.

She scowled at him. "Is that your idea of gratitude after traveling with the infidels after all these years?"

"Not at all," Nax replied. "I just wanted to make sure we were both on the same page."

"The same page," she echoed. "Do you have any idea what you've done?"

"Is there a specific thing you're referring to?" Nax asked. "I've been busy since leaving."

Her scowled deepened. "You know damn well what I'm talking about."

"I have no intention of arguing against myself."

"So you acknowledge your wrongdoing."

"Not at all," he replied. "I simply know when the game is rigged and I'm choosing not to play."

"*Rigged*?" His mother got to her feet in a single, sweeping motion. "This is not a *game*."

"It certainly feels like one," he said.

"Perhaps you've forgotten our way of life here. Too much time with the *heathens*."

He shook his head. "No, I think not. My memory remains as sharp as ever."

"Really? So what explanation do you have for your behavior?"

"None that will appease you."

She made the clicking noise with her tongue again. "I would have forgiven *everything*, had you not...*debased* your-self with this female. Do you understand that?"

Nax trembled with restrained rage. "I would ask you not to speak of Grace in that manner."

"Would you?"

He flinched at her tone.

"Yes," she said. "I thought so." She paused for a moment. "What happened?"

"Again, you'll need to be more specific," Nax said. "A lot

happened and I don't think you're going to have the patience for me to recount all of it."

She raised her hand towards him as if to slap him. "I swear, Kinlin..."

Nax raised an eyebrow. "And what would that swear be exactly, Mother?"

Her opened hand turned into a fist and hovered in the air for a moment before dropping back to her side. "Your return should be cause for celebration."

Nax made a sound like a strangled laugh. "Celebration? I think we both know that even if I had any intention of coming back here, there was never going to be any celebration."

"You're still my son," she reminded him.

"And as I recall that was the primary reason I was shipped off to that small village in the first place," he said.

"So you can imagine my surprise to find out you were on board an Alliance Fleet vessel," she said.

"Yes, I can see how that might have ruined your day," he replied.

"Remarkable."

"What?"

"I would have thought you couldn't have gotten any worse," she said. "Your attitude as a child was the one reason I you sent away in the first place. But yet, here you are, standing in front of me with a tongue that's twice as bad."

"Regretting not killing me on the spot?"

She scowled at him again. "I'm not going to have you killed, Kinlin."

"Would this be a good time for me to drop to my knees in gratitude?" he asked dryly.

She turned and stepped back to the chair, but didn't

bother to sit. "However, I'm not opposed to finding a deep hole to drop you down."

"It's refreshing."

She looked back at him. "What?"

"To discover you haven't changed at all."

His mother glared at him for a moment, not saying anything. Slowly, she sat back down, composing herself. "Have you given any thought to how it made me feel to have to dispatch a representative from the royal parliament fleet to bring you home?"

"No. But I imagine you enjoyed the opportunity to overreact."

"*Overreact*? Do you have any idea what I've been dealing with since news broke that you were off planet?"

"I'm still not entirely certain how you found out in the first place," Nax said. "So no, I hadn't gotten to considering your feelings on the matter."

"You just expected that we would never come calling?" she asked. "That I would just leave you out there in that village indefinitely?"

Nax frowned. "Is that how you found out? You decided that enough time had passed so you and your entourage trekked down to the southern peninsula to pay me a visit?"

She looked at him coldly. "A Fleet medical officer by the name of Doctor James Rabkin reached out to our Department of Health requesting your medical history and any information we might have on a possible history of insomnia for you."

Nax folded his arms and chose not to say anything. His silence communicated his righteous tone far better than any words could have.

His mother gritted her teeth. "By the time I was notified

of your current location, half the newsfeeds had picked it up."

"Is this where I'm supposed to feel sorry for you?" he asked.

"I'm not asking for your pity," she said. "I simply want you to understand the situation we find ourselves in now."

"I am very aware of my situation," Nax said. "I've been forcibly taken from my home."

"*This* is your home."

"This wasn't even my home when I lived here."

She pointed at him. "You should not have been out there in the first place."

"I suppose if you had been thinking a little more clearly you could have considered dropping me into that deep hole instead of shipping me off to a sleepy village."

"Oh, it's certainly something I've had the opportunity to reconsider since learning about your whereabouts."

"Regrets are the worst," he agreed.

His mother took a deep breath. "Kinlin, I will be honest with you, I do not care that you left. It is not ideal, but in the grand scheme of things, it is not the worst thing you have done."

"I'm speechless," he replied dryly.

"However, I need you to tell me exactly what happened between you and the *female*."

Nax pressed his lips together tightly. "The *female* has a name."

"Yes, that part I already know," she replied. "And it doesn't matter."

"It matters to *me*."

"But it doesn't matter to *me*," she replied. "And I'm still the Queen and you're still my wayward, troublesome son. So you're going to answer my questions and I'm not going to throw you in the dungeon. Are we clear?"

"Absolutely," he said. "Go ahead and throw me in the dungeon. Or, if you'd rather, go ahead and have me executed. Either one would be preferable to answering any of your questions."

She stared at him, confused, and slowly shook her hand. "Have you lost your mind?"

"Close enough," he replied. "I lost my heart."

"Not over this female, I hope."

"She's *dead*," Nax said. "Did you know that? She died *months* ago. Long before you even found out I was gone. Long before you even learned of her. She's *dead*. You're making this entire fight over a dead woman. Does this feel like a good use of your time?"

There was a cold look in her eyes. "Is there a child?"

The question startled Nax so much that he actually took a step back. "What?" His voice was a whisper.

His mother leaned forward. "A *child*, Kinlin."

Nax didn't respond. He stared numbly at the floor. A child? The notion struck him as so alien, so bizarre and yet so...right?

She gave an impatient sigh and got to her feet again. "Did you procreate with this *female*?"

He looked back up, still unable to speak.

Standing behind his mother, Grace had reappeared, smiling.

8

USS DEFIANCE

"What are you thinking?"

Mitchell looked up from the glass of Backlon brandy in his hand. Rabkin sat on the other side of the desk in Mitchell's quarters. "I don't know."

"Bullshit," Rabkin said and knocked back the rest of his brandy. "You're thinking about whether not it's worth trying to get Nax out of there."

Mitchell frowned. "If you know the answer to the question, why do you bother asking, old man?"

"Because you need to hear it out loud so you can decide if it's as dumb as you think it is."

Mitchell finished his glass. "It's dumb to want to protect a member of my crew?"

"Of course not," Rabkin said. "It's dumb to want to pick a fight with an allied planet and either get yourself blown up or the rest of the Alliance in a stupid-ass war over one Fleet officer who lied on his background check."

"Jim, it's a lot more complicated than that."

Rabkin jabbed a finger at him. "That's exactly the point."

"I can't leave Nax there to be executed," Mitchell said.

"His mother is the damn Queen. She's not going to kill her son. I don't care how much of a tight-ass royal bitch she is."

"Well, if we do go in there, I'm leaving you on the ship, because you're definitely going to get us into a war."

"What's the long-term plan if you go after Nax?" Rabkin asked. "He can't stay on the ship. You're going to hide him somewhere?"

"He can request asylum," Mitchell said.

"Asylum?"

"Why are you saying it like it's some mythical place that only fairies and space unicorns can visit?"

"Because we both know that the UPA isn't going to grant him asylum," Rabkin said. "They're going to turn him right back over to the Natuzzi. And why shouldn't they? He broke Natuzzi laws. Sure, we might think they're stupid laws, but as long as we get a promise that they're not going to execute him...Well, you and I both know damn well that the UPA doesn't really care past that."

"So what am I supposed to do?" Mitchell asked. "Because I can't leave him there."

"Sure you can," Rabkin said. "You don't even have to take the responsibility for making that decision. You're under *orders* not to do anything."

"Orders," Mitchell echoed. "They haven't stopped me before."

"You think going after Nax is worth getting knocked back down to an ensign on sanitary duty?"

"I think somebody needs to be there in his corner," Mitchell said. "Is that too much to ask for?"

Rabkin shrugged. "I don't think so. You certainly don't. The Natuzzi, though? They obviously have different priorities than we do."

Mitchell picked up his empty glass and twirled it around in his hand. "So what's your suggestion?"

"That's the beauty of just being the ship's CMO," Rabkin said with a little smile. "I don't have to make any suggestions in situations like this."

"Nax is still your patient," Mitchell said. "He could be sick."

"He sure could be," Rabkin agreed. "But, unfortunately, I don't really know a damn thing about Natuzzi physiology, much less any secret diseases they have. So that's not a move that's going to help anyone."

Mitchell put the glass back down and held out his hands. "So what am I supposed to do?" he asked again.

Rabkin took a long minute to finish his drink. Once it was empty he carefully set the glass back down on the desk. He crossed his legs and folded his arms. "Well, obviously you need to go get Nax."

Mitchell glared at him. "You're an asshole."

"I just wanted you to realize how stupid it was going to be," Rabkin said.

"Stupid or dangerous?"

"In this situation is there much of a difference?" Rabkin asked. "The man's a member of your crew and they're going to throw him to the wolves because he liked to get a little freaky with a woman outside his species? That's some grade-A bullshit right there."

Mitchell got to his feet, shaking his head. "You're a real pain in the ass, you know that?"

"I surely do." Rabkin stretched back in his seat, wincing a little as his old bones creaked. "You don't seem too bothered by it, though. You keep denying all my retirement requests." He twisted around in his seat and looked at Mitchell, who was now standing at the window staring out at the empty space on the other side of the Natuzzi border. "Has it occurred to you that had you let me retire, Nax might not be in this position? If I wasn't here, I wouldn't have reached out to the Natuzzi Health Department about Nax's insomnia and they wouldn't have known that orange bastard was out here."

"First thing that popped into my mind," Mitchell replied.

"Yeah? Make you feel a little guilty at all?"

"Nope."

Rabkin turned back around in his seat. "And people call me a bastard."

Mitchell massaged the side of his hand. "Warrick says if we shutdown decks six and seven, he can transfer power reserves to the main engines and the ion cannons."

Rabkin thought about it for a moment. "You want to make a Suicide Run?"

"It's certainly an option," Mitchell said. "The Natuzzi have limited resources when it comes to ships. We could grab Nax and be out of the sector before they got one of their cruisers up to speed."

"Still, there's a reason they call it a Suicide Run. You'd still need to send a landing party down to the planet to get him," Rabkin said. "That's going to take some time."

"Yeah."

"And you don't know where he is," Rabkin said.

"Yep."

"And, of course, there's the big one: The minute we set foot in Natuzzi space, the Natuzzi are going to know about it and before you know it, Perlman's going to be jumping down your ass."

"Yeah."

"So we're right back where we started."

Mitchell sighed. "Yeah."

The comm chirped.

"Go for Mitchell."

"Captain?" It was Sadler on the bridge. "We have a visitor."

Mitchell turned away from the window and looked at Rabkin, who had a matching expression of confusion. "A visitor?"

"*The Solomon* just dropped out of hyperspace."

Rabkin arched a bushy eyebrow. "Well, that can't be good."

9

NATUZZI

"A CHILD," Nax echoed. He stared numbly at Hawkins who stood behind his mother's chair.

"Yes, I believe you're familiar with the concept. Offspring. The result of the male and female of the species combining their DNA to create a unique being," his mother said. "In this particular instance, the child would be a product between you and the female."

Nax rubbed his hands over his face. "No. There was no child."

His mother breathed a sigh of relief and visibly relaxed. Her shoulders slumped and she sat back in the seat. "Thank our ancestors for small favors."

Nax looked at Hawkins. The grin on her face was inscrutable. He moved his gaze back to his mother. "Small favors?"

She frowned disapprovingly. "Please tell me you're not so far gone you don't realize the implications of you procreating with a non-Natuzzi female."

Nax ran a hand across his bald head. "Of course not."

His mother took a deep breath and flexed her hands on the armrests. "Well, this makes this a little easier."

"I'm glad I could help," he replied, sitting down on the edge of the bed.

She scowled at him. "I am trying to *help* you."

Nax met her gaze. "If you were trying to help me you wouldn't have brought me back here."

"You have a greater responsibility to your people," she said. "Every action you make has a consequence, an effect on our home."

"I don't want that responsibility. It's why I left in the first place."

"It's not something you can simply toss off," she said.

"And yet, I did."

"No, you didn't." His mother leaned forward on the seat. "There are going to be repercussions from you gallivanting around the galaxy with that pagan harlot that we might not feel for *years*. Natuzzi children are going to be hearing this story in the newsfeeds for weeks and it will be years, *decades*, before we have any understanding of what kind of effect it will have on them."

"Because God forbid any Natuzzi child should want something different," Nax replied.

"Exactly."

"I was being sarcastic."

His mother got back to her feet. "I wasn't." She pressed her hands against her outfit, smoothing it out. "I knew that we were going to have problems as you got older. I'm not naive. I knew you were going to be different. But this..." She gestured absently with her hands. "This is beyond the pale. You have violated the very fabric of our society. And as my son, your violations carry a weight of validity that will threaten to destroy so many of us."

"I fell in love with a woman," Nax said.

Her lips pressed together tightly. "You'll not say that again outside of this room."

"I won't desecrate her memory."

"But yet you won't give the same care to your own *people*."

"I don't particularly like my people, much less love them," Nax replied. "So, no."

She shook her head. "You're still a foolish child, refusing to listen to your elders."

"My elders sound like monsters."

Pain flashed behind her eyes. "Why do you have to make this so difficult?"

"I was perfectly content in the life I had," Nax said. "You're the one who dragged me back here."

"Content?" she echoed. "The report of your own Doctor Rabkin suggested you were struggling emotionally, possibly mentally."

"I was suffering a loss," Nax said. "And I would rather suffer that loss a thousand more times before being brought back here."

"*Loss*? Do you even hear yourself?" She gaped at him. "You speak of this female as if she was your *equal*."

"That's because she was."

His mother growled in frustration, smacking her hands together so loudly that Nax flinched. "You are such a *foolish idiot*! What is wrong with you that you cannot understand the very basic fabric of the universe?"

Nax didn't answer for a moment. "I've given a lot of thought to that lately. Grace's death shook loose something inside me that I was not aware of."

"And what, pray tell, was that?"

"Doubts. Questions. Concerns that perhaps we, as a species, were wrong."

"About what?"

He looked at her with cold determination. "Everything."

"That's heresy and if you speak those words outside of this room, I won't be able to protect you from that punishment."

"There's a man on the *Defiance* who likes to speak of convictions," Nax said. "He's pointed out more than once that if you are easily swayed, then obviously you weren't very convicted."

"It's almost like you want to die," she said.

"I won't lie," Nax replied. "I sometimes wonder if I have much to live for anymore."

"My son..." she sighed, shaking her head. "This is not what I wanted for you."

"What you wanted was for me to spend the rest of my days in that quaint little village," Nax said. "Not bothering anyone, not causing any trouble, not rocking the proverbial boat."

"And it would have been a good life."

"Not for me."

She made that clicking noise with her tongue again. "I'm so disappointed in you."

"I've been aware of that since the day I understood that I was your son and not your daughter."

She jerked back as if she had been slapped.

Neither one of them spoke for a moment. They stared at each other, wallowing in their silent rage.

Eventually, Nax spoke and asked, "What will happen now?"

She pressed her lips together and quickly regained her regal stature. "Well, obviously, you're not leaving again." She took a breath. "At this point, it's unlikely you're ever going to leave the planet again."

"So I'm imprisoned."

She rolled her eyes. "Yes, Kinlin. You're going to be confined to an entire *planet*. What a tragedy. Anyone else in your position and they would be dead."

Nax glanced briefly past his mother, but Hawkins had disappeared again.

"She's dead," he repeated.

"It doesn't really matter," she said. "It wouldn't matter if she was alive. You desecrated yourself and your people by consorting with her. I should have you executed. It would be the cleanest solution."

"Don't let me stop you."

"I'm not. You're still my son and I still love you."

Nax looked up at her. "You have a funny way of showing it."

"I have a responsibility to our people, too," she said and for a brief moment, her expression softened. "I will do what I can, but there will be certain groups that won't be happy. They're going to use this as an opportunity to attack me."

"If you're expecting me to feel sorry for you, you'll be waiting a long time," Nax replied.

His mother sighed. "I don't expect anything from you. Not now. Maybe not ever. There's a fine line between resistance and open rebellion."

"And where do I fall on that line?"

Her gaze hardened again. "Too close to the wrong side." She turned to leave.

"What's to stop me from leaving again?" Nax asked.

"What's to stop you?" She turned back to face him. "For starters, you won't be leaving the palace unattended. In addition, your face and story have been plastered all over the newsfeeds for the last forty-eight hours. There's no one on this planet that would be willing to smuggle you out for fear of getting caught themselves. And lastly, while I won't have you executed now, if you attempt to leave again, my son, the guards have been instructed to shoot you on sight."

Nax smiled grimly. "There's nothing quite like a mother's love."

"No there isn't," she agreed and stepped out of the room.

Nax looked around the empty room, but there was no sign of Hawkins.

"A child," he said out loud. "*Our* child."

Still Hawkins didn't appear.

Nax closed his eyes and dropped back on the bed. "What a thing that would have been."

10

USS DEFIANCE

"GAVIN, YOU FORGOT SOMETHING." Captain David Foster's smug face was perfect for punching. His black hair was slicked back and he had the confident air of a man who was captaining a top-of-the-line starship.

"David," Mitchell greeted him with barely restrained patience.

On the monitor, Foster chuckled. "You don't know what I'm talking about."

"Presumably it has something to do with the shuttle you just sent over without clearance," Mitchell replied. He stood outside the airlock, waiting for the seal to lock and the safety indicator to switch from red to green.

"Don't be an asshole, Gavin," Foster replied. "I'm doing you a favor."

Mitchell clenched his fist and pressed it tightly against the bulkhead. It was a remarkable show of restraint, considering he wanted to shove his fist through the screen and into Foster's face. "I'm in the middle of something here. I don't have time for your games."

Foster dropped the genial act. "I know exactly what

you're in the middle of. I'm actually bringing you two things."

The safety indicator finally switched to green and the airlock door slid open. A tall, lanky man with blond hair and a long face stepped out.

"I'm delivering your new first officer," Foster continued, "and a warning: Don't go breaking any interstellar extradition treaties. I'm just around the corner and I don't have a problem with following any orders that will keep the UPA from falling into an unnecessary conflict."

"Thanks," Mitchell said, with zero gratitude in his voice and cut the connection before Foster could say anything else.

"Permission to come onboard, Captain?" Broderick Cooper shifted his duffel and held out his hand to Mitchell.

"I could say no," Mitchell said.

"You could," Cooper agreed.

"But then you're just going to go back to D'Ambra and tell him that I wouldn't let you onboard."

Cooper dropped his hand. "I don't work for President D'Ambra."

"But you were handpicked by him to be my new first officer," Mitchell said. "How am I supposed to interpret that?"

"I don't know," Cooper replied. "Sounds like something that's above my pay grade."

"If you're a part of my ship, you're a part of my crew," Mitchell said.

"As I understand it, that's how this has worked since the early water-bound Earth vessels."

Mitchell frowned. "Are you always this sassy to your new commanders?"

"Just matching your energy, sir."

Mitchell didn't respond to that.

Cooper stood about two inches taller than Mitchell. His limbs seemed unusually long for his body. He was lean and clearly took care of himself. His face had a rigidness to it, as though he didn't smile or laugh very often. His blond hair was kept short and his face appeared freshly shaved. His dark eyes were narrow and focused on Mitchell with a calculating look that seemed neither positive or negative.

Finally, Mitchell extended his hand. "Fair enough. Welcome aboard, Commander Cooper."

The two men shook hands.

Before Mitchell let go, he briefly tightened his grip and said, "If I find out you're here to spy on me or my crew and are sending back secret reports to D'Ambra or anyone in his administration, I will not hesitate to toss you out the nearest airlock."

Cooper didn't flinch. He simply extracted his hand from Mitchell's without any fuss and replied, "You don't make a lot of new friends, do you, Captain?"

"No, I do not." Mitchell turned and started down the corridor.

Despite his longer gait, Cooper had to hurry to catch up.

"What did Foster say to you?" Mitchell asked.

"That he couldn't believe you forgot your new first officer before you left the *Atlantic*."

Mitchell shot him a look over his shoulder.

"If you're referring to whatever situation you're currently in the middle of, Captain Foster didn't fill me in," Cooper said.

"Huh."

They reached the lift and Mitchell punched at the call button. The doors opened immediately and Cooper followed Mitchell in.

"Bridge," Mitchell said and the lift started moving up.

"Bridge?" Cooper echoed.

"You have someplace else to be?"

Cooper looked down at the large duffel bag he was still carrying. "Well, I was hoping to get settled in first."

"I was hoping to not have my helmsman taken into custody by the Natuzzi government," Mitchell replied. "We're all learning to live with disappointment today."

"Ah." Cooper nodded, a knowing look on his face.

"So Foster did say something."

"No, but I heard some chatter among the *Atlantic* staff about the Natuzzi vessel," Cooper said.

"Did you take any time to read up on my crew?"

"Yes I did."

"So you're familiar with Lt. Commander Nax's situation?"

"Well, I was as familiar as anybody else was prior to the revelation that he's a member of the Natuzzi Royal Family and currently in custody for treason."

They rode the lift in silence for a few minutes.

"You playing a game here, Commander?" Mitchell asked.

Cooper kept his gaze focused on the doors. "No, sir."

"Sounds like you're playing the 'I'm Dumb, But Not Really' game."

"Not familiar with that particular one."

Mitchell looked unconvinced. "Right."

"What are our orders?" Cooper asked.

"Our orders are not to enter Natuzzi space without direct orders from the Admiralty itself."

"That seems sound."

"I'm sure the Fleet Admirals will rest well at night knowing that you approve of their decision."

"Permission to speak freely?"

"Sure, why not."

"Seems to me I'm not the only one wearing sassy pants today."

Mitchell shot him a look out of the corner of his eye.

The lift arrived at the bridge before either one of them could say anything else.

"Status update," Mitchell said, stepping out onto the bridge.

Sadler got up from the command chair. "The *Solomon* just left."

"Best news I've had all day," Mitchell said, grabbing the back of his chair.

Sadler looked from Mitchell to Cooper who still stood at the back of the bridge near the lift and then back to Mitchell.

Mitchell pointed over his shoulder with his thumb. "Everybody, meet Commander Cooper. He's the new XO. Commander Cooper, this is everybody."

"Thank goodness," Sadler said.

Cooper raised an inquisitive eyebrow.

Sadler walked up to him. "You're the new me. Or, I was the old you." She extended her hand. "Commander Sadie Sadler. I was keeping your seat warm. Now that you're here, though, I can go back to being the nightshift commander and stop having to worry about things like duty rosters and whether or not I'm going to get stuck in command again in the middle of a hostile engagement because the captain gets snatched away to some parallel dimension."

Mitchell clapped his hands loudly. "Okay, everybody. We've still got a situation on our hands. Let's stay focused on coming up with a solution."

"For what, exactly?" Cooper asked.

Mitchell turned around to face him. "I'm not leaving my crewman to face false charges of treason."

"All due respect, Captain, we have our orders." Cooper set his duffel bag down in a corner out of the way. "There's no solution for us to figure out."

"Oh boy, here we go," Sadler muttered quietly and took a step back.

"I have a crewman trapped behind enemy lines and direct orders not to go after him," Mitchell said. "Sounds like a problem to be solved to me."

"Except that Commander Nax isn't behind enemy lines," Cooper said. "The Natuzzi are an Alliance member in good standing. He's a citizen of the Natuzzi society and subject to their laws. We would be committing an act of war if we were to go after him."

A tense silence fell across the bridge. All idle conversation came to a halt. Officers were afraid to even breathe too loudly.

Mitchell folded his arms. "Are we going to have a problem here, Commander?"

"That depends on whether or not you're going to order your crew to commit an act of treason," Cooper replied, unperturbed by Mitchell's intensity.

The ensign at the comm station yelped loudly, startled by a loud beeping noise.

Mitchell turned to her and she blushed red as she checked her console.

"Captain, I have an incoming transmission from Admiral Wanamaker," she said, her voice practically squeaking. "It's coded Alpha Six-One."

"Send it to my office." Mitchell pushed past Cooper as he stepped across the bridge to his office that was set on the far side of the comm station.

"Captain, as your second-in-command, and considering our current situation, I believe I should be present on this call," Cooper said.

"And what's your security clearance, Mr. Cooper?" Mitchell asked.

Cooper paused before answering. "Twelve-B."

Mitchell nodded. "As I'm sure you're already aware, a message coded Alpha Four or above requires at least Level Ten clearance."

"And as I'm sure you're aware, as captain of this ship, you have the authority to grant security clearance up to Level Six without prior approval," Cooper replied smoothly.

The doors to Mitchell's office slid open and he stepped inside. He gave Cooper a cold smile before the doors closed. "We're going to get along real well, aren't we?"

The doors slid shut before Cooper could respond.

11

"How's the new guy?" Wanamaker asked with a shit-eating grin.

"The new guy's already accusing me of ordering my crew to commit treason," Mitchell replied.

"Sounds like the two of you are off to a great start."

On the monitor, Wanamaker's image flickered slightly.

"You need to get him off my ship, Phil," Mitchell said.

"I couldn't keep him off your ship, so I doubt I'm going to have much luck in getting him off," Wanamaker said, leaning forward. There was a five o'clock shadow on his face and he had the look of a man who hadn't gotten much sleep lately. "You've got bigger problems anyway."

"I'm not going to be able to help Nax if Cooper's going to try to get me thrown into the brig every time I make a command decision he doesn't agree with."

Wanamaker made a dismissive wave. "Have a little more faith in your crew. What do you know about Nax?"

"Hopefully less than you do," Mitchell replied. "How the hell did this slip past you?"

"Nobody's perfect."

"That's not what you go around telling everybody."

"Everything in Nax's file seemed legit and airtight," Wanamaker said. "I had three different intelligence experts vouch for him."

"And none of them knew about his status as a member of the Natuzzi Royal Family?"

"Nobody knew about it because Nax didn't want them to know about it," Wanamaker said. "What part of a Natuzzi being extremely adept at privacy are you having difficulty with?"

"Fair point," Mitchell conceded.

"Look, I'm not happy about it either and if I wasn't busy trying to keep D'Ambra from dismantling our network of security, I'd probably be more embarrassed by it," Wanamaker said. "Perlman spoke with you?"

Mitchell nodded. "The Fleet's official position is that we're hands-off and Natuzzi can do whatever the hell want to with Nax."

"Yeah, well, on the upside, I have it on good authority that the Queen isn't interested in executing him," Wanamaker said. "However, public opinion feels very differently. Thanks to the Natuzzi's infamous privacy, none of their newsfeeds are aired outside of their space. According to my sources, though, Nax's face is plastered all over them."

"What are they playing?"

"The story that he was shacking up with an Earth woman and in the process violating the very essence of what it means to be a Natuzzi. So, while the Queen isn't looking to execute him, there's an extremely large segment of the public that wouldn't mind seeing him strung up by his balls."

"Wonderful," Mitchell muttered.

"In addition," Wanamaker continued, "there are a

handful of factions within the Natuzzi government that see this as an opening to overthrow the current administration."

"*Overthrow*? What the hell is going on over there?" Mitchell asked.

"Well, apparently beneath the peaceful, xenophobic veneer is a lot of pent-up hostility that's itching to get its bloodlust on."

"This is a damn nightmare," Mitchell said. "There has to be somebody in the Admiralty that thinks it's a bad idea to just leave Nax there."

"If they do, they're keeping it to themselves," Wanamaker said.

"Wait a minute. You said *sources*. What kind of sources do you have on Natuzzi?" Mitchell asked.

Wanamaker paused before answering. "The kind I don't like to talk about over open channels."

"This is a secured comm."

"Nothing's as secured as I'd like these days."

"Now you're just sounding paranoid."

"It's not paranoia if they're really after you." Wanamaker took a breath. "There's a comet about four hours from your current location. You should be able to intercept within the next two hours."

Mitchell checked the data Wanamaker was sending him. "This is Ahines' comet."

Wanamaker's expression was neutral. "Yes."

"Phil..."

"Not on this channel, Gavin." He held up two fingers. "Two hours."

The monitor went dark as Wanamaker severed the connection.

Mitchell sagged back in his seat. "Shit."

12

"Helm," Mitchell said, stepping back out onto the bridge. "You should have new coordinates on your screen now."

"Aye."

"Best possible speed," Mitchell said as he sat down in the command chair. "I want to be there within the next two hours."

The helmsman nodded and there was a low hum as the ship jumped to hyperspace.

"These are coordinates for a comet that seems to be maintaining a circular path in and out of Natuzzi space every six cycles," Cooper said from his new station.

Mitchell slowly turned his command chair around to face Cooper. "Yes. And?"

"Given our current situation I can't imagine that's coincidental," Cooper said.

"Then maybe you don't have a very good imagination." Mitchell turned back to the viewscreen.

"Captain, if you don't mind me asking, what's our objective in regards to this comet?"

"Right now that's above your pay grade," Mitchell replied.

Cooper stepped down next to Mitchell's seat. He lowered his voice slightly. "Captain, all due respect, but I can't do my job if you're not going to keep me in the loop."

"Well, Mr. Cooper, it's my job to decide if you need to be kept in the loop." Mitchell glanced at him. "Make of that what you will."

"Sir, if you plan on taking this ship into Natuzzi space against direct orders-"

Mitchell turned to fully face Cooper. "Mr. Cooper, how long have you been on my ship?"

"Less than an hour."

"Less than an hour." Mitchell nodded. "And do you think you're making a good first impression by constantly questioning my every order?"

Cooper clasped his hands behind his back. "It's always been my understanding that a good first officer provides a necessary counterbalance to the captain. I won't do you any good if I'm just a Yes Man."

"I'm not looking for a Yes Man," Mitchell said. "I'm looking for somebody who knows how to do their job without trying to pick a fight with me every five minutes."

"If you're interpreting my behavior as an attempt to pick a fight-"

"Then you probably need to learn how to better present yourself," Mitchell said, cutting him off.

Cooper stiffened and his face set into a hard grimace.

"I understand you need to settle in." Mitchell gestured to the duffel bag. "Why don't you go do that, Commander. I'll let you know when I have the time to have a more detailed conversation on the workings of my ship."

At first, Cooper didn't move and it appeared he was

going to push the issue. Again, everyone had fallen silent on the bridge and despite the lower tone of their conversation, every officer was following along with bated breath.

Then Cooper slowly exhaled. "Yes, *sir*."

He turned sharply and walked back up to lift, pausing to grab his bag.

As soon as Cooper had disappeared into the lift, Mitchell turned back around to the viewscreen, briefly catching Sadler's eye.

"He seems nice," she said.

13

Cooper stepped into sickbay and found himself up against an immovable object.

"Can I help you?" Zemble grumbled.

Zemble towered over most of the members of the *Defiance* crew. He stood at a hair over six and a half feet tall and the horns atop his forehead tended to take that to nearly seven feet if he was standing particularly straight. So he was used to having to look down on most of his crewmates. With Broderick Cooper, however, they were nearly eye-to-eye.

It took Cooper a second, mostly because he hadn't been expecting to run into the large Elwat in the middle of sickbay. His gaze flicked to Zemble's badge, as though double-checking the rank and department signifier before speaking. He didn't need to bother, though. After all, the *Defiance* only had one Elwat officer onboard.

"Lieutenant Zemble," Cooper said.

"I know who I am," Zemble said, taking a moment to eye Cooper's own badge and rank signifier. "I'm more curious about who you are."

Cooper frowned. "I'm the ship's new first officer, Commander Cooper."

A momentary look of surprise flitted across Zemble's face. "I wasn't aware you were already on board."

"I just joined," Cooper said. "The *Solomon* had to drop me off after Captain Mitchell forgot that I was supposed to be coming on board at the *Atlantic*."

Zemble grunted. "Welcome aboard then."

"Right. Well." Cooper cleared his throat and started to move past Zemble, clearly intent on heading for the patient rooms in the back.

Zemble pivoted slightly, moving back in front of Cooper. "Doctor Rabkin isn't currently here."

Cooper's face was pinched in mild frustration. "Thank you for sharing that with me."

"Neither is Doctor Dheer."

"Well then it's good that I'm not here to see either one of them."

"If you don't mind me asking then, why are you here?" Zemble asked.

"You make it a habit of questioning your superior officers, Lieutenant?"

"Just the new ones," Zemble replied."

Cooper took a deep breath and exhaled slowly. "I didn't take this assignment uninformed."

"Good for you."

"Is this kind of casual insubordination normal for this crew?"

"Captain Mitchell doesn't mind his officers speaking their minds."

"To the point of being rude?"

Zemble shrugged his massive shoulders, but didn't say anything.

"I can't say that I appreciate it so far."

"Well then, when you get your own command you'll have an opportunity to run your crew however you see fit," Zemble replied.

"I still outrank you, Lieutenant."

"I'm aware of how the command structure works," Zemble said.

"And yet…"

Zemble shook his head. "There's nothing else. You seemed to be under the impression I didn't understand how the command structure worked and I wanted to assure you that I was more than familiar with it."

Cooper sighed and rubbed the bridge of his nose. "As I understand it, there's a member of the crew who's currently in a coma."

Zemble's face remained neutral. "And?"

"Is there something specific you're looking for, Lieutenant?"

"Just a story that makes sense," Zemble said. "As I understand it, you don't have a background in medicine."

"And?"

"And it makes me wonder what your reason is for visiting Ensign Calloway. You're not going to be able to give a second or third opinion, You're not going to be able to offer any new suggestions for care. So what exactly are your intentions in regards to seeing her?"

"Well, seeing as I do outrank you, I don't believe I'm required to explain myself to you."

"You understand that makes me a bit suspicious."

Cooper looked at him coolly. "That sounds like a problem on your end, rather than mine."

Zemble didn't say anything for a moment.

"I'm not looking to make any enemies, Mr. Zemble,"

Cooper said. "But I'm also not interested in making any new friends either. If you've got something you want to say, by all means, say it. Apparently, that's how things work around here anyway. But know that I'm not going to hesitate to have you thrown in the brig if you cross my path."

"And what, if you don't mind me asking, constitutes as crossing your path?" Zemble asked.

Cooper pointed at him. "Keep that up and you'll find out."

"Interesting hill to die on," Zemble said.

"You caught me on a bad day," Cooper said. "And I'm not a good enough of a man not to take it out on my subordinates."

Zemble grunted. "Fair enough, I suppose." He nodded with his chin towards the patient rooms in the back. "Calloway's in the third room."

"Thank you." Cooper turned and quickly made his way to the third room without so much as another look back.

He wasn't sure what he had expected. The report had been strangely vague and specific all at once. Calloway had been presented as an intriguing weak link in Mitchell's crew, but then she disappeared from the active duty roster before Cooper had even left Earth. The official report was that she was in a medically induced coma. The intel that he had been supplied with suggested otherwise. Yet standing there, looking at the young woman just lying on the bed, Cooper wasn't certain what that was even supposed to mean.

He glanced at the monitor above her. Zemble was right. He had no background in medicine, but he knew how to read vitals and hers were just...fine.

Cooper frowned and checked it all a second time and then a third. There was no reason Ensign Calloway shouldn't be awake right now.

Except she wasn't.

He reached out to touch her and his hand stopped short, hovering just above the back of her own hand.

There was a soft vibration in the space between their hands. It was almost imperceptible and, for a second, Cooper thought he was imagining it.

But, no. It was there. It was...

Something.

He pulled his hand back sharply and turned to leave. He was startled by Zemble's presence in the doorway.

"Discover anything interesting?" Zemble asked.

Cooper swallowed and struggled to regain his stoic composure. "No. What are you doing?"

"Obviously I'm watching you," Zemble said.

Cooper pushed past him, heading for the corridor. "You make it a habit to spy on your fellow officers?"

"Just the ones that I think are acting weird," Zemble replied, following after him. "What do you know about Calloway's condition?"

"Just what's in the reports." They stepped out into the corridor. "What do you know?"

"A lot more than that," Zemble said.

Cooper shot him a sideways look.

"But we both know you're not cleared for any of it," Zemble said.

"I'm the second highest ranking officer on this ship," Cooper said.

"Which means there's still at least one officer above you."

"Is everybody on this ship going to be actively working against me?"

Zemble shrugged again. "I can't speak for anyone else."

"But yourself?"

"Haven't decided yet," Zemble admitted. "So far I don't really like you."

"Nobody usually does."

"That bother you?"

"Hasn't yet."

"Good for you."

14

NATUZZI

Nax found himself trapped in a new kind of prison: one of unfulfilled possibilities.

He lay there on his childhood bed, running through it over and over again.

A *child*.

Their child.

Grace had never expressed any interest in becoming a mother and, for that matter, the thought of becoming a father had never even crossed his mind before the moment his mother had raised the question. The Natuzzi notion of fatherhood was antiquated at best, insulting at worst.

Nax had had no relationship with his own father. In fact, he had only known of his father in a very sterile, technical sense, as the man who had contributed to Nax's conception. Beyond that, Nax's father was simply irrelevant.

This had not been a problem. At least, not when he was growing up and for many years after. The strength of the matriarchy on Natuzzi was to the detriment of the male population. As such, the men had no purpose within the ruling families and, unless they were of royal blood, were often discarded back into the masses after making their genetic contribution to create any necessary offspring.

Nax's father had not been of royal blood. He had been produced because the Queen needed to conceive an heir to the throne. When the result was Nax instead of a desired female heir, Nax's father was released from any further duties of procreation and a new mate was found to help sire who would eventually become Nax's half-sister.

Remarkably, the Queen had not aborted Nax.

He did not know if this was because they had discovered his gender too far along in the pregnancy or perhaps it was something more sentimental. Regardless, she decided to keep him, birth him and raise him, despite Nax ultimately having no place in the family. Her behavior, however, over the years had made it clear that she struggled with regrets regarding this decision.

So parenthood was something of a poisoned chalice in his mind.

And yet...

A child.

A son perhaps.

Or maybe a daughter?

Nax tried to wrap his mind around the idea. It seemed too big. It felt like something impossible to imagine. But clearly, though, it was a concept even his own mother had been able to conjure up.

So why hadn't it occurred to him?

He ran through his memories, scouring every conversation between him and Grace he could think of. Perhaps there was something he was missing, something that would help better frame this notion for him.

He couldn't recall Grace ever speaking much of her own parents and even less of her childhood. Not that he was one to judge. But in all fairness, he was the one who had been trying to hide his past.

Nax sat up and looked around the room.

It was still empty.

Grace hadn't returned.

Why hadn't she come back?

"Is there something about a child that scares you?" he asked aloud. "Is there some secret you're afraid will slip out if you're here right now?"

He felt like an idiot almost immediately.

It wasn't really Grace. It couldn't be.

And if it was...

Nax shook his head as if to scatter the thought. If it was really Grace then he was going to be damned for all eternity and that wasn't something he could deal with right now.

So if it wasn't Grace, what was she?

If she was simply a figment of his own imagination, then what did it mean that she wouldn't appear now? What subconscious reason could he have for not wanting to see her now?

Fear was the obvious answer. Fear was the thing that was almost always lurking beneath the conscious mind, influencing every decision, big or small.

But if it was fear, then what was he afraid of now? What was different now that hadn't been different before?

The answer seemed almost so obvious that he nearly laughed out loud.

"Now I see you as a mother," he said. "And I can't be haunted by the dead mother of our child that never existed."

Nax closed his eyes.

And if she wasn't a figment of his imagination?

If she wasn't Grace?

If she was something else?

He opened his eyes, half expecting her to be standing there in front of him.

But he was still alone.

"What else could you possibly be?"

There was a knock at the door.

Nax didn't bother to answer. Despite the setting being his childhood room, he knew when he was in a prison cell, and prisoners were never afforded the luxury of being able to choose who they were willing to see.

But when Nax didn't say anything, there was another knock on the door.

He arched his brow and got off the bed. He watched as the door didn't open.

At the third, almost hesitant knock, Nax finally said, "Come in."

The door slowly opened and a Natuzzi male entered.

Nax didn't recognize the man.

He was of average height and dressed in the uniform of a member of the Office of Consumer Affairs. The man's jawline seemed unusually square for a Natuzzi and there was something wrong with the way he walked that Nax couldn't figure out.

"Kinlin Nax?" the man asked.

Nax didn't respond. It seemed like a question that hardly needed an answer. Who else would be kept in this particular room at this moment in time?

The man held his hand to his chest in the familiar Natuzzi greeting, his fingers curled at the knuckles. "I'm Dal Vox."

"I would say that it's a pleasure to meet you, but you'll have to forgive me as the circumstances don't allow me to feel anything particularly pleasurable right now," Nax replied.

Vox nodded. "Of course. You seem to be doing well, yes?"

"Perhaps we can skip the small talk," Nax said. "I'm held here at the pleasure of the Queen and I doubt you're here just to keep me company. So shall we skip ahead to whatever unreasonable course of action my mother has decided upon now?"

Vox paused. His eyes flicked anxiously around the room, as if searching for something.

Nax was suddenly struck by a familiar notion he couldn't quite identify.

Vox took a step forward and seemed, for a moment, to want to move closer, but held himself back at the last moment. He lowered his voice, speaking hardly above a whisper, "Have you ever wondered why there's only one way into Tartis Four?"

At first, Nax thought he misheard.

The question seemed so out of place, so alien in the current context that he *must* have misheard.

He blinked and waited. Perhaps Vox would realize he hadn't heard correctly and would repeat himself.

Instead, Vox just stood there and said nothing as he waited for a response.

There was something in the man's eyes Nax hadn't noticed before and he realized he hadn't misheard.

But this wasn't possible.

This would be the very definition of *insane*.

If this was true and this man was...

Nax shook his head. "You're not real."

Vox was taken aback. "Excuse me?"

"You're clearly not real," Nax replied. "It's the only logical explanation."

Vox paused and glanced back over his shoulder, as if half-expecting somebody to suddenly burst through the door. He turned back to Nax. "I don't mean to be that guy, but that's not the correct response. And you're going to need to give me the correct response if you want to get out of here."

This couldn't possibly be real.

And yet...

What were the odds that he would conjure up a completely different hallucination? Especially when the first one was so personal, so intimate?

Vox stood there waiting, clearly growing more impatient by the second. "Have you ever wondered why there's only one way into Tartis Four?" he asked again.

So Nax searched his memory. It took longer than he would have cared for. But as Warrick was fond of saying, so many of their skills fell into the unfortunate category of Use It or Lose It.

And so, on the verge of losing it, Nax said, "Of course not. It's only natural because there four different ways to get into Tartis One."

15

USS DEFIANCE

THE AHINES' comet was nearly ten miles long and half as deep. Crystalized ionized particles were left in its wake as it made its way through space, giving the comet a dark blue trail that slowly faded away against the darkness of the empty void.

At just shy of two hours from Wanamaker's transmission, the *Defiance* dropped out of hyperspace and matched the speed of the comet.

Shortly after that, a shuttle was dispatched from the *Defiance* and headed for one of a dozen small cave-like openings on the comet. Its approach was cautious and hesitant, but sensors showed no indication of any potential threats.

Sensors also suggested there was nothing inside any of the cave openings that would be of any interest to the shuttle's crew. Which was, of course, the whole point.

As the shuttle entered the cave it passed through a small distortion field and almost immediately the sensors told a very different story.

On the other side of the distortion field, deep within the

center of the Ahines' comet was a small, self-sustaining base. It was large enough to accommodate exactly one standard size shuttlecraft. The interior of the base had enough air and provisions to support two or three individuals for about a week, if necessary. That could be stretched to a month for a single individual.

The sensors hadn't detected the distortion field because of the comet's ion trail. It successfully camouflaged any fluctuations from the field. Besides, the Ahines' comet was a wandering celestial body that had been designated essentially an empty, dead rock in space. Any passing ship wouldn't give it a second glance. Which, of course, was also the point.

After the airlock sealed, Mitchell and Keane stepped out into the small base.

The inside was only three rooms: There was a small living quarters, a storage unit and the communications bay. The airlock opened into the communications bay.

Keane whistled as he examined the equipment. "Half of this stuff is older than the *Defiance*."

Mitchell walked over to the main console and flipped some large, manual switches. "I think it was built from spare parts left over from when they decommissioned the last Heinlein class ship about thirty years ago. It's probably the only way Wanamaker kept it off the books."

Keane opened the silver doors on the north side of the communications room. He found a small bed and a kitchen unit. Adjacent to the kitchen unit he noticed there were two more cots folded up against the wall. Keane stepped back and the doors slid closed. He moved to the other door that was across from the airlock where he found basic supplies and a small surplus of weapons.

"All the firepower in here is pretty new, though." Keane picked up a plasma rifle. It had that polished, brand-new, factory fresh look to it. He racked the slide and checked the power settings. The rifle hummed in his hands. He flipped it over to check the make and model under the barrel. "Damn. This is a Wacem Forty-Five. These aren't even out yet. The last report I read said the Fleet wouldn't be getting any of these until next year and even then, they were only going to be distributed to Galaxy class ships. It looks like Wanamaker's got at least three crates of them here. In addition to quantum grenades that only just started being distributed three weeks ago!"

There was a squeal from the speakers in the communications room as Mitchell adjusted the settings on the console. "Phil likes to be prepared."

"This isn't just being prepared," Keane said. "This is like...Hell, I don't know what this is like."

"This is like actually having a budget to work with," Mitchell said. "Over half of this stuff was probably ordered at least two years before D'Ambra took over. There's no way Wanamaker could get any of these orders slipped through now."

Keane held the Wacem rifle in a shooting stance and checked the sightline. "Think anybody'll notice if I take a few back with us?"

"This isn't a shopping trip," Mitchell said.

"Well, sure." Keane powered down the rifle and set it back on the rack, almost regretfully. "That's why I asked you if anybody would care if I took it."

Keane stepped back out in the communications room.

The main screen had lit up and the Directive Fifty-Two logo was on it.

"Here we go," Mitchell said. He glanced at Keane briefly.

"Try not to look like a fat kid scheming to steal all the candy."

Keane pressed a hand against his chest in mock injury. "Captain, you wound me. I'm a professional spy. If I don't want anybody to know that I'm scheming, they're not going to know."

Mitchell grunted and turned back to the screen. "Then maybe you should wipe that grin off your face."

Before Keane could respond, the Directive Fifty-Two logo disappeared and Wanamaker took its place.

"Well, how's it going?" he asked.

"I think I'm supposed to be asking you that question," Mitchell said, leaning back against a chair that was mostly metal. "What the hell am I doing on a dead drop base that's on an orbit that takes it in and out of Natuzzi space on a regular basis?"

Instead of answering, Wanamaker looked at Keane. "Commander, you're looking well."

Keane eyed his captain for a second before responding, "I feel great."

"Any side effects?"

"Of dying and then being miraculously restored by an alien entity from a higher dimension?"

"Unless something else of note has happened to you recently."

Keane shook his head. "Well, if you're wondering if I've grown any extra limbs or a taste for human flesh, neither has happened."

"Right. Because those are the only things to worry about," Wanamaker said.

Keane just shrugged.

Mitchell twirled an impatient finger. "Phil, let's get to the point here."

Wanamaker grumbled cantankerously under his breath. "Well, it should go without saying, but what I'm about to tell you is extremely classified and extremely sensitive. Which is why I couldn't trust the information over a coded channel."

"This sounds like it's going to be juicy," Keane said.

"Gavin, as you'll recall, I recently spoke with you about intel on the Veneer situation, received from an undercover source."

"Yeah, it sounds familiar," Mitchell said flatly.

Wanamaker fidgeted. "You'll also recall I didn't feel comfortable telling you where this source was located, beyond the fact that they weren't in Veneer space and that we had no exfiltration plan in place."

"I changed my mind," Keane said, growing dread in his voice. "I think I see where this is going and I really don't think it's going to be the kind of juicy I was looking for."

"You don't know the half of it," Wanamaker said.

"Shit," Mitchell said. "You've got somebody on Natuzzi."

"I've got somebody on Natuzzi," Wanamaker said.

Mitchell smacked the console in frustration. "What the hell, Phil?"

Wanamaker jabbed his finger at Mitchell. "Hey, watch it."

"What are you going to do, Phil?" Mitchell asked. "I've already got a new first officer who's looking for an excuse to toss me out the damn airlock."

Wanamaker glowered at him. "Maybe I'll give him a good excuse."

Keane held up a hand. "Wait a minute. I just want to be clear about this: You're actively spying on a UPA member? One of our *allies*."

"I'd hardly call them an ally these days," Wanamaker said.

"Either way, it's still illegal under the UPA security charter," Keane said.

"Which is why it's extra problematic," Mitchell said.

"Sure. *Problematic*," Keane said. "Let's call it that."

"It's a position we wouldn't be in if the Natuzzi weren't so damn secretive," Wanamaker said.

"Well, speaking as a member of a top-secret organization," Keane said. "They might have a good reason."

"Doubtful," Wanamaker replied.

"How the hell did you get somebody onto Natuzzi in the first place?" Keane asked.

Wanamaker sat back, folding his arms. "It was complicated."

"Complicated?" Mitchell echoed.

"Do you want me to give a breakdown of how this worked, or do you want to hear about how it's going to help you?" Wanamaker asked.

"How it's going to help *me*?" Mitchell looked unconvinced. "Right now it looks like one of *your* messes that you need me to clean up."

"The two aren't mutually exclusive," Wanamaker said.

Mitchell rubbed his tired face. "You know, everybody's always warning me not to start any interstellar wars. But I'm starting to think *you're* the one they need to be talking to."

"If you don't mind me asking, what's this agent doing on Natuzzi in the first place?" Keane asked. "And how the hell is he getting intel on the Veneer Empire?"

Wanamaker shuffled some things around on his desk. "Apparently the Natuzzi aren't as sheltered as we've been led to believe. About eight months ago I received intel suggesting the Natuzzi were sending representatives into their neighbor's back yard."

The image on the monitor split into two. On the right

was Wanamaker, and on the left was a map of Natuzzi space and the border it shared with the Veneer Empire. Three planets were highlighted.

"These three locations were Veneer mining colonies," Wanamaker continued. "Or at least, that's what we were led to believe. They were among the first of the Veneer locations to go dark right before their home world followed suit. Long-range sensors picked up two separate ion trails that our analysts identified as Natuzzi vessels about a week after these colonies went dark."

"What were they doing out there?" Mitchell asked.

"That's what I wanted to know," Wanamaker said. "Which is why I sent an agent to Natuzzi."

"And what did this agent find, Phil?"

"That the Natuzzi are keeping very close tabs on what's going on with the Veneer Empire, or what's left of it," Wanamaker said. "Why, though? No clue. To be fair, it's not a bad idea. The Veneer Empire is in disarray and they're literally next door to the Natuzzi. You could argue the Natuzzi are just being cautious by keeping an eye on the situation. Hell, it's the same thing we're doing."

"But presumably nobody's got a spy within our organization trying to figure out why we're doing it," Keane pointed out.

"Well, sure," Wanamaker said. "But we also don't have a long history of staying out of interstellar affairs and going out of our way to not go anywhere. You know how many ships left Natuzzi space in the last twelve months? Three. And that includes the one that took Nax."

Mitchell looked at the graphic again. "And that number doesn't include any of these ships."

"No it does not," Wanamaker said. "So on top of all that, the Natuzzi don't want anybody to know they've been popping over the border. Which, of course, makes me even more curious as to what they're up to."

"And your man on the inside?" Keane asked.

"He's got plenty of intel. But it's got no form, no substance. It's empty, description documentation. There's nothing behind any of it that suggests why the Natuzzi are behaving like this."

"How long do you think your man can keep this up?" Mitchell asked. "If the Natuzzi find out we've got somebody there…"

"Yeah, yeah," Wanamaker said. "The shit'll hit the proverbial fan." He sighed. "My man needs out. The update he passed along on one of the Ahines' comet's last orbital cycles suggested that the climate on Natuzzi was rapidly changing and not for the better."

Mitchell shook his head. "I don't see how this is supposed to help anybody, Phil."

"It's going to help avoid not one, but *two* interstellar incidents," Wanamaker said. "My man needs to get off Natuzzi and Nax needs to get out of there before somebody changes their mind and has him executed. Nax is public enemy number one right now. My guy is literally a nobody in the system."

"And how am I supposed to get the Defiance close enough without setting off alarms in both governments?" Mitchell asked.

"In eight hours the Ahines' comet is going to pass by a small Natuzzi scout ship that's holding a stationary position just inside the Satinal nebula. Normally you'd have to space-walk the jump, but seeing as you've got the shuttle resources that my man doesn't, it should be a little less exhilarating."

"Okay, let me make sure I've got this right," Keane said. "You want us to hang out on this dead drop base until we meet up with your stolen Natuzzi vessel. Then we take the ship to Natuzzi Prime where we're presumably going to rendezvous with your agent and Nax, neither of whom any of us have been in contact with, because this base would be the only way for us to pass a message along to your agent in the first place. But, somehow, we're supposed to meet up, get them off the planet and then make our way back to the *Defiance*."

"I didn't promise it was going to be easy," Wanamaker said.

"Sure," Keane replied. "But there's a big difference between 'easy' and 'needlessly complicated'. Plus," he looked at Mitchell, "there's still the question of what the hell are we supposed to do with Nax? Cooper's going to notice two Natuzzis suddenly on the ship."

"I have faith you'll figure something out," Wanamaker said.

"That's it?"

"What do you want from me? A list of potential disguises for the two of them?"

Keane shrugged. "It's not a bad place to start."

Wanamaker shook his head. "Gavin, the clock is ticking. The longer this takes, the less likely either of our guys gets out of there."

Mitchell nodded. "Roger that."

Wanamaker gave him a tiny salute. "Best of luck, old friend."

The screen went dark.

"Shit," Mitchell muttered.

"Yeah," Keane said. "You know, Wanamaker's man could have made this move at any point. They've got the system in place."

"Yeah, so?"

"Except that if he made it all the way out here, well, he'd have nobody to meet up with him," Keane continued. "Because since D'Ambra started his witch-hunt, Wanamaker's scuttled a bunch of the Directive Fifty-Two resources. We're the closest ship, but even we would need an excuse to get this close to the Natuzzi border, given how skittish they are about maintaining their privacy. So..."

"So what?"

Keane shrugged. "Are we sure Wanamaker's not the real reason Nax got dragged back to Natuzzi? You have to admit, it's awfully convenient. There's a lot of moving pieces that all happened to click into place at the same time. Nobody's going to question why the *Defiance* is out here, especially when her captain has a history of breaking the rules to help his crew."

Mitchell didn't answer for a moment. He just stared at the old console, watching one of the lights blink on and off.

"No," he said finally.

"No, what?" Keane said.

"Sometimes it's just a happy accident, Commander."

"Okay. Sure. A *happy accident*. Let's call it *that*."

Mitchell just shook his head. "Come on, let's figure out a cover story to keep Cooper off our asses."

16

COOPER SAT in the command chair, uncertain of what his next move should be.

On the surface, Mitchell's story seemed plausible.

It wasn't out of the realm of possibility that the shuttle suffered minor engine failure by passing through the comet's stardust trail. In fact, such a thing had been documented to have happened in the past in similar situations.

But in this particular situation, it didn't feel quite right.

Cooper turned the chair around, looking for somebody on the bridge and his gaze immediately fell on Sadler, who was pointedly trying not to look at him.

He got up and walked over to her station, adjusting the sleeves of his uniform as he went.

"Commander," Cooper said quietly, leaning his back against her console.

"Yes, sir." Sadler cleared her throat. "How can I help you?"

"Obviously, I'm new here."

"Sure, obviously," Sadler agreed.

"I haven't even been assigned quarters yet," Cooper said.

"Do you want me to-"

"No, that's not my point," he said. "I'm using that to illustrate my point. Which is, that perhaps there's something I'm missing, what with being the new guy."

The corners of Sadler's mouth turned downward slightly and she shook her head in confusion. "I'm not sure I follow."

"The captain detours us to this comet." Cooper gestured at the image of the Ahines' comet on the viewscreen. "Offers no explanation as to why we're suddenly investigating it. Upon arrival, instead of dispatching a science team, he and Commander Keane take a shuttle over to the comet. Then they suffer engine failure while inside one of the caves of the comet. Repairs are to take approximately sixteen hours. And when I offer to send assistance, the captain refuses. What am I missing here?"

"I think it's fairly obvious," Sadler said. "Captain Mitchell is a very prideful man and he doesn't really want to accept help from the new guy."

Cooper mulled this over for a moment. Again, on the surface, it made a kind of sense. But...

"No."

"I'm sorry, did you just say *no*?" Sadler asked.

"I don't think that's it."

"Well, I don't know what to tell you," she replied. "I mean, you came over here for my opinion and so I gave it to you."

"Except I don't think that's your opinion." He looked at her. "Do you know why I'm here?"

"Because the previous first officer died and we needed a replacement," Sadler replied.

"I wasn't Captain's Mitchell's first choice," Cooper said. "In fact, I wasn't his choice at all."

Sadler struggled to keep her expression fairly neutral. "I believe I recall hearing something to that effect."

Cooper nodded. "Of course. Something to that effect." He pressed his hands together and held them under his nose for a moment. "Captain Mitchell is a highly decorated officer and, until recently he was also a highly respected officer. Then some things happened and now I'm here because there are people who don't trust him."

"I'm not sure what kind of reaction you're expecting from me right now."

"I'm honestly not certain myself," Cooper admitted. He gestured at the viewscreen. "But this is the sort of thing that isn't going to help Captain Mitchell. Because if nothing else, you're right: It makes him seem like a selfish, prideful son of a bitch."

"Well, sure," she said. "But you can't toss him in the brig for being a selfish, prideful son of a bitch."

He stared at her for a second, almost surprised. "No, I suppose you can't."

"Commander Cooper," the helmsman spoke up.

"Yes?" Cooper asked, straightening up from Sadler's console.

"The comet's current trajectory is going to take it back into Natuzzi space within the hour."

"Oh, is it?" Cooper didn't exactly sound surprised.

"Should I plot a course to follow?"

"Absolutely not," Cooper said, stepping back down to the command chair. "We were given explicit orders not to enter Natuzzi space. So Captain Mitchell is going to be on his own while he deals with the unfortunate timing of his engine failure."

Cooper sat back down and glanced back at Sadler, but she was, once again, pointedly not looking at him.

17

NATUZZI

"You're not real."

Vox frowned and looked genuinely concerned. "That's the second time you've said that. I hope you can understand why I find that concerning."

Nax pressed the tips of his fingers together and moved slowly around Vox in a circle. "Admiral Wanamaker would have to be insane to devise an op like this simply to extradite me from my home planet."

"Well, sure," Vox said, scratching his nose. "But that's not why I'm here."

Nax stopped walking and just stared at Vox. "I beg your pardon?"

Vox glanced back at the door again. "We don't actually have a lot of time here."

"Then I suggest you speak quickly."

"I'm not here to, well, rescue you," Vox said.

"Yes, so you mentioned already," Nax replied. "If time is of the essence, repeating facts I'm already aware of isn't going to help."

"I'm here on a different assignment," Vox said.

Nax narrowed his gaze. "A different assignment?"

"I don't think repeating what I've already said it going to help move this along."

Nax gave him a withering look, but didn't say anything.

"I was dispatched here eight months ago to investigate the Natuzzi's interest in the Veneer Empire."

The last few pieces clicked into place and Nax went from mildly confused to aghast with horror. He took a step back. "You're not a Natuzzi."

Vox gently gestured with his hands in the universal symbol of 'keep it down.' "Let's not go around announcing that too loudly."

"My mother would have you shot on sight."

"Which is why I don't want her to know, obviously."

"Wanamaker's gone insane," Nax whispered.

"Let's also not use specific names like that," Vox said. "I'm fairly certain your room isn't bugged, but using names is going to get us both into a lot more trouble than we need right now."

"More trouble than an undercover Directive Fifty-Two agent spying on Natuzzi soil?"

Vox glared at him. "What the hell did I just say?"

Nax pressed his lips together tightly and didn't say anything for a moment. He glanced at the closed door as if expecting it to burst open suddenly.

Nax flicked his gaze back to Vox. "What are you doing here?"

Vox sighed irritably. "I told you: I'm investigating the Natuzzi's interest in the Veneer Empire."

"No." Nax gestured with the first two fingers of his left hand at his room. "What are you doing *here*? I'm not connected to the Veneer Empire, and this is the first time

I've been back home in fifteen years. I'm not going to have any useful, actionable intel for you."

"Ah. Right," Vox said a little sheepishly. "Well, that's true. Here's the thing. Well, actually, it's *things*. First: I need help."

"Again, I would like to refer to my previous statement." Nax looked him over carefully and was unable to see anything that would suggest that Vox was not a natural Natuzzi. "Also, you seem to have a handle on your situation."

"Well, that's because I'm all about faking it 'til I make it." Vox grinned and it was a decidedly non-Natuzzi grin. "That being said, there's some individuals in the Intelligence Department that have become...suspicious of me."

"If they were suspicious that you're an off-worlder spy, you'd be dead already," Nax said.

"That's why they think I'm actually working for one of the factions that are looking to destabilize your mother's government."

Nax narrowed his gaze again. "And why would they think that?"

"Because that's what I want them to think," Vox said. "It clearly buys me more time."

"Until they realize you're not connected."

"Well, sure. Hence the ticking clock," Vox replied. "There's no such thing as a lie that won't end up exposed."

Nax frowned. "That's a particularly discouraging point of view for an individual in your line of work."

"If I anticipate that everything's going to blow up in my face, I can make preparations to dodge the explosion."

"You've been here for the last eight months, what could I possibly help you with?"

"You can help me try to dodge the explosion," Vox said. "Your mother's been sending expeditions across the border into Veneer space since before their home world went dark."

Nax look at him, puzzled. "Why?"

Vox shrugged. "Nothing in the intelligence reports suggests any kind of motive and, clearly, I'm not going to get into any kind of position where I'll be able to gain her confidence."

Nax quickly ran through everything he could remember about his mother. "Taking into account that before today I hadn't spoken with her in nearly twenty years, I can't imagine a scenario where my mother would be interested in establishing any kind of diplomatic relations with the Veneer."

"Except there's no Veneer for the Natuzzi to connect with," Vox explained. "Now that the Veneer Empire essentially no longer exists, everything's being run by the Oxean Syndicate. Your mother's had an offer from Syndicate representatives at the border."

"Never mind my mother," Nax replied. "Natuzzi society as a whole wouldn't negotiate with the Veneer Empire, much less a criminal terrorist organization like the Oxean Syndicate."

"Except where do you think we've been getting all our intel on what's been going on behind the Veneer borders?" Vox asked. "I've been basically copy/pasting it right from the intelligence reports that are being filed here."

"What's your working theory?" Nax asked.

"Expansion."

"The Natuzzi government isn't interested in expansion," Nax said. "We never have been. We are quite content with what we have."

"That was before the empire next door went supernova."

"The UPA would frown upon it," Nax said. "Without any

actionable intel, that space is still occupied by an independent governing organization. This would be tantamount to staging an invasion."

"Maybe," Vox agreed. "But right now the governing organization is the Oxean Syndicate."

Nax took a moment to think it over. "You want me to speak with my mother."

Vox made a face. "Oh, hell no. That would be even worse than me trying to gain access to the Queen. What basis would you have for talking to her about this?"

"Then what kind of help do you think that Natuzzi's prodigal son can provide?"

"I need access to the Sicurezza Vault," Vox said.

Nax closed his eyes, placing his hand over his face. "Of course you do."

"If there's anything they're trying to hide from prying eyes, it's going to be kept in there."

"Typically, yes, this is where the Natuzzi government maintains anything that would be considered highly classified," Nax said. "Being that it's one of the most highly secured locations on the planet, walking into the Sicurezza Vault you might as well wear a sign that says you're a spy."

Vox nodded. "Sure, that's going to be a problem. But before I get to *that* problem, I have the problem of getting *in* to the Sicurezza Vault."

"You can't get cleared because you can't subject yourself to the necessary DNA testing."

Vox nodded. "However, all the Royal Family members have access to it."

Nax drew still. "My access will have been revoked."

"Actually, it hasn't."

Nax blinked in surprise. "I'm sorry?"

"Your mother has, obviously, restricted you to the palace.

But, she hasn't actually revoked any of your clearances, security or otherwise."

"That doesn't seem very likely," Nax said.

"Yeah, sure," Vox agreed. "It sounds like a pretty big oversight. But look at it from their point of view, your disappearance, reappearance, and subsequent treason have all basically occurred within days of each other. Yeah, you're public enemy number one around here, but it hasn't occurred to anyone that you should be treated as such. Now, that's not going to last much longer." He pointed in the direction of the window. "You're not a popular figure out there and the way you're being prominently featured in the newsfeeds, it's eventually going to occur to somebody just like it occurred to me, and when they check your file, they're going to discover the same thing I did. At that point, your mother will have to revoke all of your permissions, just to save face and, even then, we both know that at the rate this is going, it's not going to help her much. Either way, once that happens, you can't help me and I can't help you, and we're probably going to both end up dead. At this point, best case scenario, we're probably looking at hours before that happens."

"And what do you hope to find in the Vault?" Nax asked.

He shrugged. "I don't know. I'm just following a hunch, making sure I tick all the boxes."

There was something in Vox's eyes that gave Nax pause. "No, there's something specific you're looking for."

Vox took a deep breath and slowly exhaled. "Do you recall a public figure by the name of Dalin Kel?"

Nax thought about it for a moment. "Yes, vaguely. I remember he was a community organizer for the Ramun Valley District."

"Since you've been gone he's moved up in the world,"

Vox said. "About three years ago he started a movement to have Natuzzi males recognized as equals among the women."

"Well intentioned, if not a little foolhardy," Nax said. "He'd be fighting centuries of status quo."

"And he was doing it rather successfully," Vox explained. "In the first year he got enough public support he was able to get the issue of equal pay on the next voting cycle."

"That's...impressive," Nax replied.

"The people like him. The establishment, not so much."

"And when you speak of factions working against my mother..."

"He's one of the biggest right now."

"That's very impressive," Nax said. "Given he's fighting against an establishment that could have squashed him like a bug."

"The Queen thought it was important to let his voice be heard. She quickly regretted that. See, it's not just that Kel wants representation for the men in Natuzzi society, he's trying to play the same script, but flipped. A lot of his big ideas, at their core, are just the same things your family's been doing since they got into power."

"A friend of mine once said there's no such thing as new ideas," Nax said.

Vox turned grim. "When the Auxiliary Judicial Department sponsored two new judges for the West Frineft District, Kel and his group ran a smear campaign that resulted in one of the candidates being assassinated the night before they were going to be sworn in. Kel quickly distanced himself from it, claiming it was the action of a lone wolf, but it's impossible not to see his fingerprints all over it."

"Then why hasn't my mother brought him to justice?"

"Because she gave him too much freedom in the beginning and he's a voice in the system," Vox said. "If she goes after him, she would be looking at an armed revolt in the Ramun Valley, Little Leot and Fippiak Districts."

"Not that I'm in favor of it, but she has the entire Natuzzi army at her beck and call," Nax said. "It would be fairly easy to make quick work of those three districts."

"Dominos," Vox said. "Once those three go down…"

Nax nodded. "Seg West and Ciorreonas Center follow."

"And before you know it, Natuzzi's in the middle of a civil war," Vox finished. "Which is why I think your mother has been relying on the Sicurezza Vault. Thanks to his position, Kel has access to almost everything in the Intel Department, but he won't have clearance to the Vault."

"And you suspect my mother is using something from the Veneer or the Oxean to take out Kel without plunging the planet into a civil war?" Nax asked.

"I think the Queen made a mistake a few years ago and is trying her best to not repeat it," Vox said. "There are blank spots in the Queen's schedule. They don't look like blank spots, of course. But I've been studying them and the activities she's supposed to be engaged in don't exist."

"That seems sloppy for my mother."

"The events are scheduled and then retroactively canceled after the fact. They're all private events with family and conveniently, nobody ever thinks to question any of the family she's supposed to be meeting with. But once the event is retroactively canceled, it doesn't really matter. The end result, though, is a blank spot in her schedule that happens to match up pretty closely with the Sicurezza Vault Director's private schedule."

"They simply could be engaged in an affair," Nax said. "My mother is known for choosing lovers of convenience."

Vox winced at that. "Okay, well, that's a possibility and not exactly one I wanted to talk about with the Queen's son."

"I'm simply making sure you're covering all of your bases," Nax said. "Assuming what you've said is true, what's the second thing?"

"Second thing?"

"You said there were essentially two reasons why you were here," Nax reminded him.

"Right. Yes. Two." Vox nodded. "Well, the second thing is: If you stay here, you're definitely going to end up dead."

18

As if on cue, Hawkins reappeared.

She stood next to Nax and whispered into his ear, "I don't know if you should trust him."

Nax managed to keep his gaze maintained on Vox. "As I'm sure you can understand, I find that to be a questionable statement. My mother has already assured me she won't be seeking the death penalty." He struggled to maintain his composure as Hawkins ran her fingers along the base of his neck.

Vox moved to the window to check the horizon. "The Queen isn't the one you have to worry about."

With Vox's back to Nax, he turned to face Hawkins. She gave him a mischievous look.

"What? Is it something I said?" she asked, laughing softly when he didn't respond. "You want to know why I don't think you should trust him? Just nod your head for yes."

Nax didn't move.

She pouted. "Party pooper."

"If anybody makes an attempt on my life against her

wishes, they'll be tried for treason themselves," Nax said, turning back in Vox's direction.

"Yeah," Vox replied, pressing his hands against the window as he leaned forward to get a better look at the ground below. "That'll be real comforting to you once you're dead."

"I've made peace with my actions," Nax replied.

"Good for you," Vox said. "I still need your help and I would imagine there are a bunch of people who aren't on this planet that would very much like you not to end up dead."

"And then there's me," Hawkins said. "I'd like you not to be dead, too. And, really, when you think about it, I'm kind of the one who matters the most."

"Let's be honest here, they can't let you live," Vox said.

"Who?"

"Everybody," Vox said. "The establishment, the anti-establishment and everyone in-between. Sure, the Queen told you she wouldn't execute you, that doesn't mean she won't stop somebody else from pulling the trigger."

"That's exactly what it means when the Queen says it," Nax replied.

Vox turned back to him. "Not in this instance and you know it. If they let you live, they're essentially validating all of your actions."

"That's a stretch," Nax said.

"It's the kind of stretch people are willing to make," Vox said. "There's no resolution to the problem that is you that doesn't result in your death."

"He's laying it on pretty thick, don't you think?" Hawkins asked.

"So I'm not getting off this planet alive," Nax said.

"That's not entirely true."

"What does that mean?"

"I think it's fairly self-explanatory," Vox said.

"He's not wrong," Hawkins whispered.

"You have a way off-planet?" Nax asked.

Vox paused. "Not exactly."

"Not exactly?" Nax echoed.

Vox made a face. "It's...complicated."

"How complicated?"

"Complicated enough that I don't feel like wasting my time explaining it if you're not onboard with me."

Nax looked around his childhood room.

"Oh, come on," Vox replied. "What's there to think about? If you stay here, you *die*. If you come with me, there's a possibility you don't end up dead."

"That's a hell of a sales pitch," Hawkins said sarcastically.

Nax still didn't respond.

"You've already been found guilty of treason," Vox told him. "It's not like a little more treason is going to make much of a difference."

Finally, Nax turned back to him. "You are doing a terrible job of convincing me."

"Well, sure, usually I like to take my time and finesse a subject," Vox said. "But like I already pointed out, I'm on a timetable here and I'd rather not waste any more of it."

"Pressuring you to make a rapid, uninformed decision?" Hawkins made a *tsk* sound. "That's textbook manipulation right there."

"I'm not sure what's the difficult decision here," Vox said impatiently.

"The end result seems to be the same, regardless of what I decide," Nax said. "Either way I end up dead. At least if I stay here, perhaps I can pass in peace."

Vox stared at him. "What the hell is wrong with you?"

"I'm having an existential crisis," Nax replied. "I've been dragged back to my home planet to face charges of treason for falling in love with an off-worlder who's now dead."

"I get it. I have bad days, too."

"Well, now he's just being an asshole," Hawkins said.

"But I don't contemplate suicide every time things don't go my way," Vox finished.

Nax bristled. "It's hardly suicide."

"If you're letting people just kill you without putting up some kind of fight, it's suicide," Vox said. "End of story."

"Then perhaps you shouldn't bother with trying to recruit me as it's not going to be particularly helpful to you to have a suicidal partner," Nax said.

"I'm not going to lie, you wouldn't be my first choice," Vox said. "But it's not like either one of us has a wealth of options to choose from." Vox pointed at him. "If nothing else, you swore an oath. That should count for something."

"I've sworn many oaths," Nax replied. "And most of them were before I joined the Fleet and Directive Fifty-Two. So if it's a question of loyalty, I'm afraid you're going to have to get in line."

Vox was starting to get impatient. "Damn, you're a stubborn bastard."

"He ain't wrong on that," Hawkins said. She moved between Nax and Vox.

"So I've been told."

"We don't have time to discuss this ad nauseam," Vox said. "I've already put a lot more effort into this than I thought I was going to have to."

"My apologies," Nax said.

"I don't want your apologies. I want to know if you're in or out?"

Nax looked at him and then turned to Hawkins.

She smiled at him and waved her fingers. Something in the gesture made Nax think of a child. Specifically, their child that never existed.

The smile dropped from her face.

"That's not fair," Hawkins said. "You can't blame me for something that never happened."

And yet...

Nax considered what the rest of his life was going to be like and whether or not it was going to be worth carrying this burden with him until his deathbed.

"It doesn't have to be a burden," she said. "I don't know how many times I have to say this. *We* can be in this *together*."

A brief image of his mother flashed in his mind. As always, she was composed of disappointment and anger. He couldn't recall of a time when he had seen her smile at him.

"And is that something you want to punish me for?" Hawkins asked. "Or yourself?"

He nodded slightly and turned back to Vox.

Vox started to visibly relax.

Nax said, definitively, "I'm out."

19

THE UNEASY SILENCE in the room was broken by a soft beeping.

"Shit." Vox reached into his robe and pulled out a small device. "Shit."

"What is it?" Nax asked.

"I set a tripwire alarm before I came in here," Vox said as he checked the signal on the device. "Anybody who was heading in this direction and less than ten feet out would trigger it."

"That seems overly cautious," Nax said.

"Not really. I don't have a good cover story for being here with you."

Nax pursed his lips together. "I'm beginning to wonder why you were selected for this mission."

"Because I'm very good at improvising." Vox slipped the device back into his robe. "Mind you, I have a cover story. It's just not one you're going to be very happy with."

Nax's brow furrowed. "How so?"

"It's the kind of thing you're going to have to roll with before I explain it to you."

"I don't like the sound of that."

"Well, it's not going to get any better." Vox paused and pulled out a fusion pistol from a hidden holster. "Sorry."

In less than three steps, Vox had positioned himself slightly behind Nax and had the fusion pistol pressed against Nax's temple.

Nax wisely chose not to move. "I'm failing to see how this plan is going to help you."

"Wait for it."

The door burst open and two palace guards swept into the room.

"Your Majesty, by order of-" The guard stopped abruptly as he quickly became aware of the situation. He immediately unholstered his weapon.

"That's not a good idea," Vox said. "Not unless you want the Queen's firstborn to have his brains splattered across this room."

The guards hesitated. But there was something in their hesitation that did not give Nax any comfort.

"I want you both to listen to me very carefully," Vox continued. "Are you listening?"

The first guard tightened his fingers around the grip of his weapon, but didn't raise it. "We're listening."

"Good. Because this is going to be very important." Vox paused and then exclaimed, "*For freedom of men!*"

Then he shot both of them.

The guards dropped to the ground.

The air in the room sizzled from the fusion pistol's shots.

"Now we're really on a timetable." Vox pushed passed Nax and grabbed the sidearms of both guards. "I disabled the palace sensors before coming here, but that's not going to last much longer. Honestly, I spent more time talking to you than I thought I would have to." Vox checked each guard's pulse. They were alive but stunned unconscious. He nodded, happy with his work. "Okay. Good." He straightened up. He gestured at Nax with the pistol. "Come on."

Nax didn't move. "I'm failing to understand the nature of your plan here."

"My plan is for the palace to think that a representative from Kel's Freedom Movement kidnapped you," Vox said. "See, I told you you weren't going to like it."

"This is the cover story you concocted for why you would be seen with me," Nax said.

"Like I said, it's not ideal."

"Indeed." Nax agreed. "As there's still the problem of me not going with you."

"Well, to that I would say two things: One, if you stay here, how exactly are you going to explain this," he gestured to the unconscious guards, "without blowing my cover? You may be suicidal and struggling with the point of your existence right now, but I'm betting you don't want to toss me to the wolves for no reason."

"The reason, in this case, would be because you were unable to conceive of a plan that was less likely to blow up in your face," Nax said.

Vox ignored him. "And two," he pointed the pistol at Nax. "I'm willing to do more than just playact this bit."

Nax frowned. "Shooting me seems counterproductive to your plan."

Vox nodded. "Sure. Like I said, it's not a great plan. But it's doable. As long as I don't shoot you in either leg, you should be able to move fast enough for us to get down to the Vault before people come looking for you."

"I find it hard to believe that you would-"

Nax didn't get to finish because Vox fired off a shot that passed dangerously close to his left ear. In fact, it was so close Nax felt the ambient energy sizzle burn him ever so slightly.

"I figure you only need one good ear to hear me," Vox said.

"I could just stand here and let you shoot me until I'm dead," Nax replied.

Vox glared at him. "You're a special kind of stubborn, aren't you?"

Nax didn't bother to respond as the answer seemed self-evident.

"At this point, you either come with me or shit is going to get very bad not just for you and me, but everybody else, too. Because if my cover's blown, do you know what kind of fallout there's going to be? Is that something you want on your conscience as you go off into whatever afterlife you people believe in?"

Nax paused for a moment and glanced back over his shoulder, looking for Hawkins. But, once again, she was gone. He turned back at Vox. "Fair point."

"Yeah, I thought so."

He gestured impatiently with the fusion pistol. "Let's go before the next people who show up actually want to kill you."

20

NATUZZI

Vox and Nax sloshed through wastewater that was nearly ankle-deep. The sewer tunnels that ran under the palace were made from blossombrass stone and the red hue of the walls seemed to eat up the light of Vox's flashlight.

"This is disgusting," Hawkins said, trailing just behind Nax. She had reappeared after they entered the sewers. "I'm reconsidering your decision to die that's how disgusting this is."

Vox paused at a Y-junction and checked the map on his scanner. "This way." He gestured left.

Nax wordlessly followed.

"I hope you don't expect to spend any intimate time with me later," Hawkins said. "Because you're going to need a chemical bath before I'm willing to touch you again after this."

Something sloshed in the murky water around their ankles.

"Oh, I'm definitely going to be sick," Hawkins said. She moved closer to Nax. "You know, you can't trust him." She nodded at Vox who stayed about ten steps ahead. "He's using you."

"I'm aware of what he's doing," Nax murmured quietly, keenly aware of how well sound traveled with blossombrass stones.

"Then why are you following him?" Hawkins asked. "Let him die. You don't know him. You don't owe him."

"His death could set off an interstellar conflict between the UPA and the Natuzzi," Nax replied. "Hundreds of millions could die in the process."

"Not your problem," Hawkins said. "The Natuzzi called you a traitor and the UPA didn't exactly rush to have your back when your people came for you. I say let them both burn."

"That would be irresponsible on my part."

"I think you're missing my point here," Hawkins said.

"No, I understand you perfectly." Nax looked at her. "Grace would never suggest letting the universe burn out of spite."

"Well, that was before I died," she said. "Since then I have a whole new outlook on life. Pun intended."

"I can't keep doing this," Nax said.

"You say that every time. And the very next time you just keep doing it," Hawkins said. "I don't know why you're in such denial. You deserve a little happiness, you know."

"This isn't happiness," Nax replied.

"That's because you're not actually doing it," she said. "If you keep fighting it, it's always going to be miserable. Stop fighting it."

He stopped and turned to her. "And what happens if I do that?"

Hawkins gestured towards Vox. "You need to keep up.

How are you going to explain why you stopped to talk to empty air?"

"Damnit," Vox said. "We have a new problem."

Before Nax could ask what he meant, he felt the tunnels shake.

Hawkins leaned in and whispered, "Told you so."

Tiny waves began to appear in the wastewater.

"What is it?" Nax asked, his feet splashing around in the dirty water as he hurried to catch up to Vox.

"They're going to be on top of us any second now," Vox said. "Shit."

There was a loud thrumming that started in the distance and quickly grew louder as it drew closer to them.

"News broke that you're gone," Vox said. He had to shout to be heard over the thrumming. It was now loud enough that both men could feel their back teeth rattling from the noise.

"We need to *move!*" Vox shouted. He started running as best he could in wastewater that was growing deeper by the second. It was already up to their knees.

Nax followed, but kept looking back over his shoulder in the direction of the loud thrumming. The closer it got, the more distinct it became. Its echo reduced and Nax was able to identify the sound as an engine.

Vox checked his scanner again. "We're not going to make it."

"Who is it?" Nax asked.

"It's not the welcome committee," Vox replied.

Suddenly, from around the last corner they had turned, two security detail hover pads burst into the tunnel. There were half a dozen palace guards between the two hover pads. The heat from the engines filled the sewer tunnels, cranking up the temperature by forty degrees in a matter of seconds.

Nax vaguely heard one of the guards shout something and point at them.

Vox fired off a handful of shots and then started running. Nax quickly followed.

"This way!" Vox led them down another split corridor.

The hover pads gained on them too quickly though.

"We are going to need a new plan!" Nax shouted.

"Working on it!" Vox shouted back. "Here." He tossed Nax the spare gun he took from the palace guards earlier. "Cover me."

Nax whirled around and fired without hesitation.

He wounded two of the guards on the first hover pad and they went down immediately. It would have been more helpful if one of them had been the pilot, but they weren't and the hover pad continued to bear down on them.

"Okay." Vox pulled out a small round device from his robes and thumbed it on. "New plan."

He tossed the device towards the hover pads and then grabbed Nax by the collar, hauling him down under the wastewater.

Nax recognized the device as a thermal explosive and as the murky, disease-ridden water closed over him, the bomb detonated.

The explosion filled the narrow confines of the sewer tunnel, engulfing both hover pads and the palace guards.

From beneath the surface of the wastewater, Nax watched as the explosive fire rolled over them, not piercing the liquid barrier as the hungry flames ate up oxygen and lapped at the blossombrass stone walls hungrily.

After a handful of seconds that felt like years, the explosion dissipated and the two men broke the surface of the wastewater, gasping for air.

Nax pushed away from Vox, looking for something to hold for support. The walls still burned, but he didn't notice.

"You killed them," he gasped.

Vox made a futile effort to wipe the filthy wastewater from him. "I didn't have much of a choice. If I hadn't, they weren't going to take us back alive."

"You don't know that."

"Actually, I do." Vox pointed to the smoking remains. "How the hell do you think they got palace guards down here so quick? We're already halfway to the main aqueduct line. We left the palace a half hour ago."

Nax just stared at him, not understanding.

"The palace has known you've been missing since at least then," Vox said. "I'm not monitoring their feeds. I'm monitoring the *public* newsfeeds."

"You're saying my mother dispatched somebody to take care of us before the news went public," Nax said.

"The Queen or somebody else so she could have plausible deniability." Vox took a breath. "They were shooting to kill, not stun."

Nax looked back at the smoking wreckage, searching for any sign of life.

"You know how this works," Vox said.

"I'm beginning to think I don't."

"Come on." Vox started moving again. "Seismic sensors would have logged that explosion. It's not going to take a tactical genius to figure out where we are. We need to get topside."

Nax didn't follow right away. Something floated past him in the wastewater. It took him a second to recognize it as the hand of the palace guard who had pointed at them.

He looked around for Hawkins, hoping for some familiar face that could reassure him of...something.

But, of course, she wasn't there.

21

THE SOUL OF OBSESSION

DOCKED AT STARBASE ATLANTIC

"Jacoby?"

"Yes, ma'am?"

"What are your thoughts regarding us throwing a dinner party?"

The Vulderran looked up from the book he was reading in mild surprise. "A dinner party, ma'am?"

Vi'van Bendare stood at the observation window, looking out over the terrarium that was maintained by the crew of the ship she called home. Her dark, purple-skinned body was unusually covered in a thick, fluffy robe. The only parts of her body visible were her small, slender hands poking out from the oversized sleeves, and her head.

She took a sip from the glass flute she held and relished the tingling sensation of the Boveran blood wine as it slid down her throat.

"Yes, a dinner party," she repeated after a moment, pulling the edges of her robe against her even tighter.

"A dinner party or a *dinner* party?"

She glanced back at him, her eyes sparkling with

mischievous intent. "Naturally I would *love* the latter. But I don't think we could convince Kathryn to attend."

"No, I don't believe Commodore Straub would be interested in a *dinner* party." Jacoby sat on the opposite side of the room. His large, dusky, grey frame seeming unusually small in the unusually large room.

Like most Festus vessels, the room was designed to create the illusion of open space where there was none. There were no sharp corners. Walls gently blended together, curving and bending like waves.

"Yes, she can be a bit of a wet blanket," Bendare agreed, sipping at her drink. "No, I was thinking of something a little more...official."

"Official?" Jacoby echoed. "I must confess, I'm not sure I follow."

"As a gesture of goodwill," Bendare clarified. "The guest list would be small, naturally. We want to keep it intimate. Although, perhaps, not that intimate. Obviously, we would invite Kathryn. Mr. Mallozzi as well. Ambassador Lekhak is a must. No dinner party is complete without his sparkling wit. And if we must, we can include Leyla. Although we both know she is far worse than Kathryn at sucking out all the joy of an event." She sipped her glass and then lit up with excitement. "Oh! And we must absolutely invite *Cayden*."

"Commander Keane?"

Bendare nodded enthusiastically. "Yes, of course. I don't know why I didn't see this before. In fact, now that I think about it maybe it should be less of a party and more of an intimate affair between Cayden and I."

"If you don't mind me asking, ma'am, what happened to this being a gesture of goodwill?" Jacoby asked.

"I have plenty of goodwill to extend to Cayden."

"I'm sure you do."

She glanced back at him. "Do I sense a note of disapproval?"

"I think that's certainly something we could investigate," Jacoby said with his typical, diplomatic tact.

"Which is your way of saying that you don't approve."

"That's not it at all, ma'am." Jacoby got to his feet. "I'm simply thinking of our current agenda and I don't know that you want to allow yourself a distraction with Commander Keane."

"You're sweet, you know that?"

"So I've been told."

Bendare stepped away from the window and set her empty glass down on the table. "But I think we can afford ourselves a slight distraction with Cayden. After all, I think it's the kind of distraction that could bear interesting fruit."

"If you say so," Jacoby said.

"You can't deny the man's story has a certain...appeal to it," Bendare said.

Jacoby cleared his throat. "If you'll forgive me for being a bit straightforward, ma'am, but have you taken the time to review the information provided by Fl'eu'ri'mond?"

Bendare absently trailed a finger around the edge of her glass. "Yes."

"And?"

She looked at him and folded her arms so that they disappeared completely into her sleeves. "I'm more interested in what *you* have to say about it."

"In all fairness, ma'am, I'm not the boss," he replied.

"Ah, well, yes, that's true." Bendare smiled. "But that doesn't mean you aren't a valued member of my organization. Perhaps, the second most valuable, after myself, of course."

"Of course." Jacoby frowned and clasped his hands behind his back. "My thoughts are as follows: It's not worth our headache." He paused and added, "Even if it's real."

"Well, now that's an interesting twist. Even if it's real."

"The Oxean Syndicate is not exactly known for providing reliably factual intel."

"For the amount of money we're paying our source, it better damn well be based in some reality."

"And if it is," Jacoby said. "I don't know that it's something we need to be involving ourselves with. As you recall, you began this endeavor looking to expand into the untapped industry of kameko dealing."

"Which you also have hesitations about."

"I simply prefer to stick to what we know best."

"Sometimes the things we know best aren't even things that we know we can know."

"You know, I do not approve your appropriating ancient Vulderran sayings," Jacoby said. "Translating them out of Vulderran always results in a butchering that's painful for my ears and the ears of my ancestors."

"Well, they're already dead and I pay you too much to get worked up over a simple thing like that." Bendare took a deep breath and exhaled loudly. "Honestly, I don't like it either."

Jacoby looked visibly relieved.

"That doesn't mean we can't recoup some of our investment on the intel."

Jacoby's relief didn't last long. "I beg your pardon?"

"What did it cost us?"

"Half a million standard credits."

"I'm sure there's somebody we can sell the information to at, what? At least a ten percent markup? Possibly more if we can dissuade any concerns they might have about the legitimacy of this information."

He frowned. "That seems a mite irresponsible."

She waved off his concerns. "Oh, please. Who did we just sell a cache of Backlon EMG bombs to? Besides, if you're that worried about tainting our poor souls, we can start with the UPA. I'm sure they would *love* to have this intel. I seem to recall rumors of one of their agents running around Natuzzi looking for something juicy anyway. Of course, the Alliance has nice deep pockets, so maybe we'll shoot for a twenty percent markup."

Overhead, the lights flickered.

"What was that?" Bendare asked, glancing up at the ceiling.

"I'm not certain. Perhaps a power surge?" Jacoby moved to a nearby console, but before he reached it an alarm started blaring across the ship.

Bendare pressed her hands against her ears. "I don't like that!"

Jacoby reached the console. "It's some kind of intrusion alert!"

"*What*?" Bendare shouted, unable to make him out over the blaring of the alarm.

Jacoby raised his voice. "It's an intruder alert!"

Bendare winced. It felt like the alarm was piercing her brain with knives. "*Intruder alert*? Who the hell would be stupid enough to-"

Abruptly, the alarm stopped.

Bendare cautiously lowered her hands. She could still hear an echo of the alarm. "Well, that's better."

"Reports are coming in from across the ship," Jacoby said, scanning the screen. "But they're mixed. I can't tell if we're being boarded or not."

"*Boarded*?" Bendare frowned. "This was not what I had in mind when I suggested we have a dinner party."

"I imagine not," Jacoby said.

"If this is Kathryn's doing-" Bendare was cut off as the door burst open in a hail of fire.

She jolted back with the force of the explosion, slamming up against the window overlooking the terrarium. She yelped in surprise and pain, raising her hands to protect her face.

With a roar, Jacoby leaped over the console and rushed forward, moving with surprising speed for a creature of his size. The floor thudded beneath his massive feet. His hand swooped down to the holster under his arm, but it was an effort in futility.

A blast of blue energy exploded out from the smoke of the doorway, striking Jacoby across his body and jolting him up into the air. A second surge burst through the blue energy and sent him flying back across the room. He crashed back into the console and it exploded around him.

Thick smoke billowed in from the doorway.

Jacoby groaned painfully and started to get up, pieces of glass and Festus plastic crunched and crumbled beneath him every time he moved.

Another blast of blue energy exploded out from the smoke and made sure he stayed down. Yellow blood leaked out from cuts that split open across his body as the energy raked over him. A painful cry escaped his mouth.

Three figures emerged from the smoke.

At first, Bendare couldn't make out their details. Then the ship's ventilation system kicked in and the smoke began to clear.

She recognized them immediately as humans. They were dressed in black suits with a single band of white that wrapped around their collars and then extended down the center of their suits. Two of them held weapons she wasn't familiar with, which was a rather remarkable feat considering she was one of the largest black-market arms dealers in this corner of the galaxy. The weapons looked like long cattle prods with twin prongs at one end. Blue energy crackled between the prongs. One of the humans twisted the grip of their prong and the blue energy cascaded out from the prongs, spilling across the room like a mini-lightning storm.

Behind her, the window to the terrarium exploded. Bendare screamed as thick shards of glass rained down on her. She pulled herself deeper into her robe, holding her hands over her head. But she still felt dozens of cuts across her body.

The blue energy receded and Bendare cautiously glanced at Jacoby, hoping to see that he was about to get up. But instead, all she saw was the broken Vulderran lying in a puddle of his own blood.

The man in the middle of the three humans squatted in front of her. "Ms. Bendare." His hair was blond and neatly parted to the side. He reached out with his hand and gripped her chin tightly, turning her head so that he could look her directly in the eye. "We're from the Church of Eternal Clarity and we'd like to have a *word*."

22

AHINES' COMET

"Captain?"

Mitchell didn't answer. He sat in front of the console, staring at the blank monitor, his gaze distant.

"Captain?" Keane prompted again, his voice a little louder this time.

Mitchell blinked and glanced up. Keane stood off to the side, two weapons bags filled and ready. He rubbed his eyes, shaking his head. "Sorry. Lost in thought."

"We're about twenty minutes out from the scout ship," Keane said. He rapped his knuckles against the wall and they made a soft clanking sound. "This thing makes good time."

Mitchell got to his feet. "I think Wanamaker may have installed a Dalton ion engine to help keep it more regular." He nodded at the bags. "What have we got?"

"A little bit of everything. But I don't think we're going to want to shoot our way in and out."

"It's not going to be ideal," Mitchell agreed.

Keane gestured to the sleep quarters. "I also found us a

change of outfits. I don't think it'll be smart if we get caught wearing our Fleet uniforms."

Mitchell plucked his Fleet badge from over his left breast and held it in his hand as if feeling its weight.

Keane leaned against the wall, folding his arms. "If you don't mind me asking, what's on your mind, Captain?"

"A lot of stuff, Mr. Keane." Mitchell set the badge down on the console. "Remind me, when were you recruited into Directive Fifty-Two?"

"Right after the incident at Serenity Base," Keane said.

Mitchell looked at him. "Hell of an opportunity to come your way after nearly dying."

"I wasn't going to look a gift horse in the mouth."

"And now?"

Keane frowned. "I'm not sure I follow."

"What was your first field assignment?"

"Helped extradite a handful of Gurung refugees from a Backlon concentration camp."

Mitchell nodded. "Good mission?"

"We didn't lose anybody, if that's what you're asking."

"I'm asking if it was a good mission."

Keane took a moment before answering. "It was a Backlon concentration camp, so it sure felt like history was on our side."

"And was it?"

"Early on I made a decision not to follow up on any past missions," Keane said. "I didn't want to be disappointed in how things turned out after we left."

"Understandable."

"Is there something specific you're getting at, Captain?"

Mitchell gave his badge a little push and it spun in a circle on the console. "Phil Wanamaker is one of my closest, oldest friends. We came up through the Fleet together.

We've made a game out of how many times we've saved each other's lives."

"But...?"

"Directive Fifty-Two was originally born out of the initial conflict with the Unity," Mitchell said. "It had a clear mission statement: Protect the UPA against threats that were too dangerous for the public to be aware of. At the time, that seemed like a fairly clean objective. If the general public understood what had really happened with the Unity..." Mitchell shook his head. "Feels like somewhere along the line things changed. For the most part, those changes are for the better. After all, who's going to protest the rescue of refugees from a Backlon concentration camp?"

"Well, the ones we had to leave behind probably weren't very happy."

"Wanamaker didn't have this agent on Natuzzi because of the Veneer," Mitchell said. "It wouldn't be possible to get him in place with the resources that were available once the Veneer Empire started to collapse. All of the Directive Fifty-Two resources had been frozen or shut down." He looked at Keane.

"So the agent would've been in place prior," Keane said.

"An op like this would've taken at least ten months to prep, maybe longer," Mitchell said. "The agent would need at least six months recovery time from the cosmetic work needed for him to blend in."

"You're worried about why Wanamaker had an agent there in the first place," Keane said.

"It's definitely on the list."

"And what if it's just another happy accident?"

"Sometimes it's a happy accident," Mitchell said. "Sometimes it's the result of an op that's been carefully planned out and executed over an extended period of time."

"So, now what? You don't trust the admiral?"

"No, not exactly that," Mitchell said.

"So what?"

Mitchell shrugged. "You asked me what was on my mind, Commander, and now you know."

"You know, I think I prefer our relationship when you've got more answers than questions," Keane replied. "It creates an air of command that's easier to believe in."

"I'll keep that in mind," Mitchell said dryly. "Any thoughts as to what we're supposed to do once we get to Natuzzi?"

"Not yet," Keane admitted. "You?"

"One or two."

"Are you going to be able to present them in a manner that's going to be more confident than the last pair of thoughts you shared with me?"

Mitchell shot him a look.

Keane held up both hands. "You know what, that last one was totally over the line. We definitely don't have that kind of relationship yet."

"You familiar with the wing and a prayer maneuver?"

Keane made a face. "Yes. Please tell me that's not what we're doing here."

"Have you had a chance to speak with Mr. Zemble about his faith?"

"All the time," Keane said. "He doesn't shut up about it."

"Mr. Keane," Mitchell sounded slightly chastising.

"Well, he doesn't," Keane replied. "It's not like I'm saying something that isn't true."

"His faith is a rather amazing thing," Mitchell continued. "No matter what happens, it doesn't seem to falter."

"Yeah, it's kind of annoying."

Mitchell shot him a sideways glance.

Keane threw up his hands again. "I don't know what you want to hear from me, Captain."

"What I'm saying is that I believe we're going to need to have a little faith," Mitchell said. "A little faith that Mr. Nax and this agent are going to be ready for us and that things are going to go our way with as little trouble as possible."

"That's not much of a plan," Keane said.

"A wing and a prayer, Mr. Keane," Mitchell said. "It's better than nothing."

23

USS DEFIANCE

"Westin, you little piece of Fim'ai shit, are you trying to get us all killed?" Thick clouds of blue steam billowed out from the vents above the ion drive as Warrick shouted up at the second level of engineering. A blond-haired figure jumped back from the railing. He jabbed his finger up at her. "I see you!"

There was a loud clamoring noise as she raced off back to the conduit tube.

"You can't hide from me, not on this ship!" he shouted.

An alarm started blaring from the console in front of him.

Warrick frowned and turned his attention to the blaring console. "Why are you doing that?"

The console didn't respond.

Warrick adjusted the settings, but the alarm wouldn't shut off.

"Stop that." He smacked at the side of the console, but that just caused the alarm blare through engineering's main speakers.

Warrick closed his eyes and pressed his fingers against

the bridge of his nose as he took what were intended to be deep, calming breaths. "I'm going to kill her," he muttered. "I'm going to kill her and save us all in the process. They'll probably give me a damn medal."

He opened his eyes and turned around to find Commander Cooper standing there.

"Who the hell are you?" Warrick asked. "And why are you standing in my personal space?"

"Commander Broderick Cooper," he introduced himself. "I'm the ship's new XO." He pointed towards the general direction of the speakers. "Is that alarm important?"

"If it's not accompanied with a countdown, it's usually not," Warrick replied.

"That's an interesting way to run engineering."

"Well, it hasn't failed me yet," Warrick replied.

Cooper wordlessly reached around him and punched in a command code on the console. The alarm immediately shut off.

Warrick glanced back to see what he had entered and nodded appreciatively. "Okay. That's certainly one way of handling it."

"Commander Warrick, I wonder if I could have a moment of your time," Cooper said. "Assuming you're not in the middle of anything."

Warrick glanced up at the railing on the second level. "Assuming that Westin doesn't overload any more lithium circuits, sure I've got a minute or two."

Copper gestured toward an empty corner of engineering.

"I didn't know we had a new XO," Warrick said.

"I'm sure Captain Mitchell had every intention of introducing me to the crew before running off to get stuck on a comet on the edge of the Natuzzi border," Cooper said flatly.

Warrick fidgeted with the sleeves of his uniform awkwardly. "Ah. Sure."

"As I understand it, you and Lieutenant Commander Nax were good friends," Cooper said.

Warrick stopped short. "We still are," he said, giving Cooper a cool glare.

"Of course." Cooper tilted his head apologetically. "Poor choice of words on my part."

"Was it?" Warrick asked. "Because it didn't feel like it."

"Well, to be fair, the general assessment is that none of us will ever see Lt. Commander Nax again," Cooper replied. "So I figured referring to your relationship in the past tense seemed the correct way to reference it."

Warrick folded his arms. "You must be real fun at funerals."

Cooper didn't say anything for a moment. He pressed his fingertips together. "Okay, I'll get right to the point: I'm not particularly concerned with your relationship with Mr. Nax."

"Yeah, I cracked that code."

"What I'm interested in is the captain's relationship with Mr. Nax."

That caught Warrick off guard. "Captain Mitchell?"

Cooper frowned. "Does this ship have another captain I'm not aware of?"

Warrick glanced around, as if expecting someone else to abruptly join the conversation. "I'm not entirely certain what you're asking."

"I thought it was a fairly transparent question," Cooper said. "I want to know what the nature of the captain's relationship is with Lieutenant Commander Nax."

Warrick took a minute before answering. "They're not best friends, if that's what you're wondering."

"But does Captain Mitchell value Mr. Nax enough to go against direct orders from the Admiralty and risk an interstellar conflict in an attempt to retrieve him from Natuzzi custody?"

"I'm not exactly certain what the correct answer to that is," Warrick replied carefully.

"Ideally it would simply be the truth."

"Ideally the truth wouldn't get Captain Mitchell court-martialed," Warrick said.

Cooper raised an eyebrow. "Ideally, I suppose you're right."

Warrick shook his head. "I don't know what to tell you, Commander. If you're looking to build a case against Captain Mitchell, you're barking up the wrong tree."

"I'm not looking to build anything," Cooper said. "I'm simply trying to figure out what exactly is going on around here. Because, obviously, things are happening that aren't supposed to be happening."

Warrick shrugged. "I wouldn't know anything about that."

"That's not what I've heard."

"And who have you heard that from?" Warrick asked.

"People who are more familiar with you than I am," he answered.

"I'm not looking to get off on the wrong foot with you," Warrick said.

"And I'm not looking to start a fight," Cooper replied.

"And I don't think either one of us believes what the other just said."

"Apparently not," Cooper agreed.

The two of them stood there, silently staring at each other for nearly a full minute.

Blue steam stopped venting out from above the ion

engine. There was a double chime over the alert system and Warrick felt his stomach flip as the gravity in engineering dropped by two points.

"*Westin*," he growled, and pushed past Cooper. "What the hell did you do *now*?"

Cooper watched as Warrick disappeared behind the ion engine. The change in gravity didn't bother him. He hardly even noticed it. He waited for a minute. But it quickly became clear that whether or not this was a legitimate emergency, Warrick was going to use it as an excuse not to continue their conversation.

Cooper made a mental note, then left.

24

NATUZZI

"WHERE ARE WE?" Nax asked.

Vox didn't answer. He was focused on turning the metal lid above them. He grunted as he pressed into it and there was a scraping metal noise as he slowly pushed it off to the side.

Nax looked up, trying to get a view of the space beyond Vox, but it was too dark.

Vox pulled himself up through the hole and then a moment later reached down to help Nax out of the sewers.

It was darker than the sewers had been so it took a moment for Nax's eyes to adjust. When they did, he could make out the enormous size of the location, with thick pipes traversing the space around him, some nearly as thick as he was. The ground was wet stone. As his eyes got used to the dark he became aware of two giant tanks in the center of the space. There didn't seem to be anyone else nearby, but there were two sounds that caught Nax's immediate attention: A low background hum of machinery running and the gentle sloshing of water.

"It's a water processing plant," Vox said, dragging the

metal grate back over the hole. There was a loud clank as it dropped into place. "Just outside the Berdown Cove. Mostly automated."

"The Pinneak Facility," Nax said.

Vox looked at him in surprise. "You're familiar with it?"

"I used to come here as a child," Nax said. "I found it relaxing."

Vox took a second to just listen to the quiet machinery and the gentle sloshing of water. He nodded. "Yeah, I can see that."

Nax turned to him. "We're headed in the opposite direction of the Vault."

"That's the plan."

"Considering this whole endeavor is to gain access to the Vault, you're going to have to explain this one to me."

"We're creating a false trail," Vox explained.

"That they'll simply follow right back to the Vault," Nax replied.

"Did you miss the part where I said it was a false trail?"

"It's still a trail, regardless of how true or false it's intended to be," Nax said. "My mother doesn't employ fools."

"The Queen isn't the one I'm worried about right now." Vox started moving for the exit.

"So you've implied," Nax said, following him. "Who should we be worried about?"

"No offense, but I don't have time to bring you up to speed on all the new political factions working on Natuzzi these days."

"You certainly had the time back in the palace to fill me in on Kel and the Freedom Movement."

Vox glanced back at him. "And you didn't exactly seem appreciative of it."

They reached the exit and Vox punched in a six-digit security code. There was a noise as the locks slid back and the door swung open.

"That was before I realized we were going to be leaving a wake of bodies," Nax replied. "Now I would like to know at least a little something about the people we could end up killing."

"Sounds like I missed something fun."

Nax drew up short, startled.

In the empty alley on the other side of the door, under the soft glow of the Natuzzi sun, there stood a woman. Her skin was dark orange and had a healthy glow to it. She wore a casual dress and carried a thick bag made of dark yellow Agenore beast leather slung across her chest. She had the general appearance of a person on their way to a marketplace, out to do their daily shopping. But her eyes sparkled with the energy of a troublemaker.

Vox stood between them and raised a cautious hand to Nax. "It's okay. She's with me."

Nax looked back and forth between them. "With *you*?"

She waved at him. "Pleasure to meet you, Your Majesty."

"Stop it," Vox said.

"Am I supposed to be rude?" she asked.

"No names," Vox said.

"But I already know his name," she replied. "Actually, the entire planet knows his name."

"You're not funny."

"I'm a little funny."

He shook his head. "If he gets caught, I don't want you caught because he dropped your name."

She looked at Nax. "You wouldn't do that, would you?"

"I have never sold out another soul to save my own," Nax replied solemnly.

"There you go," she said.

Vox just shook his head.

Nax eyed Vox suspiciously. "You didn't mention you were working with a partner."

"That's because you don't appreciate it when I give you intel," Vox said. "And besides, she's not my partner."

"Please," she said with a wounded expression. "I should think this rates me at least an accomplice, if not an actual partner. This is treason we're committing here. The prince here is the least popular man on the planet right now."

"Stop it," Vox muttered.

Nax arched an eyebrow. "You have a sense of humor."

"So I've been told." She smiled. "Do you know that the Del Central Newsfeed ran a poll and an overwhelming seventy-five percent thought you should be executed?"

"I haven't had the chance to get caught up with the local news," Nax deadpanned.

She gave him a dismissive wave. "Don't worry about it, though."

"Oh? And why is that?" Nax asked.

"All the polls are fixed," she explained. "None of the newsfeeds actually reach out to the public at large. They simply go to the groups that will help further their narratives."

Vox glanced around, paying attention to the sky. "This is really not the time."

"They have narratives?" Nax asked.

She nodded her head. "Sure. There's no real news anymore. If it's not something that's being pushed by the Parliament, then it's something being pushed by the media. There aren't any outlets reporting on what's actually going on in the world today."

"Seriously." Vox looked at her, irritated. "This is not the time and, more importantly, he's not going to appreciate it."

"He's not?" She seemed doubtful.

"I gave him the whole rundown on Kel and the Freedom Movement," Vox said. "Trust me, it was wasted on him."

She turned back to Nax. "How long have you been off planet?"

"How long are the newsfeeds saying I've been off planet?"

"Almost seventeen years."

Nax nodded. "That's about right."

She smiled. "Hey, look at that. It's not all lies."

"Come on." Vox was getting impatient. "We need to get moving. Is the transport here?"

"Yes," she said.

"Good. Any problems?"

"No. But then, we didn't have the man whose face was plastered all over the newsfeeds," she said, as they made their way to the end of the alley. "So, you know, it might be a little different now. What happened down there?"

"The Queen already dispatched a hunter/killer team," Vox said.

She gasped.

"Except that the only people who were doing any killing down there were us," Nax said.

Vox looked back at him. "Would you have preferred it the other way around?" He shook his head. "Never mind. Don't answer."

"Why do I have a feeling the plan's not going too well?" she asked.

"What are the newsfeeds reporting?" Vox asked.

"That his Royal Majesty is responsible for the murder of several palace guards."

"That could be the reason behind that feeling of yours," Vox replied.

They reached the end of the alley which led to a sleepy street with almost no traffic and certainly no pedestrians nearby.

"I don't see a vehicle," Vox said.

"Hang on." She reached into her bag and pulled out a small communicator. "We're ready." She dropped the communicator back into her bag and turned to Vox. "I had him keep moving, so it didn't look suspicious."

"You have more partners?" Nax asked.

"I have help, yes," Vox said, pointedly not looking at Nax.

"You didn't mention any of this before," Nax said.

"As I've already pointed out, you didn't appreciate any of the information I did give you."

"None of that information seems as relevant as the details of a network in place to provide you with assistance," Nax said.

"We're not really a network," she said. "We're just a loosely connected group."

"A group," Nax echoed.

"Loosely connected," she added.

"Still a group."

She nodded. "A group of people who are trying to do the right thing."

"Stop talking," Vox said.

"What's the right thing?" Nax asked.

She shrugged. "It's complicated."

"Please stop talking," Vox said again.

She pointed at him. "He's asking questions."

"Yes, I'm standing right here," Vox said. "I hear him asking questions and I'm telling you: stop answering his questions."

"If I can't answer his questions in a time like this, then what's the point of all this?" she asked.

"I'm eager to hear the answer to that myself," Nax said.

A large vehicle came to a halt in front of them. The rear doors opened and an older Natuzzi male waved them in.

"Come on," he said. His voice was gruff. "There's a patrol about six miles out."

The three of them hurried into the vessel.

The inside was large enough to hold the four of them, plus at least two others. Although the only other individual Nax was aware of was the driver.

The older Natuzzi settled back in his seat and winced a little. He was dressed in what Nax identified as a construction worker's outfit.

"We're lucky," he said.

"I'm not feeling very lucky," Vox said, pulling out his scanner.

"They could have a curfew in place," the old man said. "We could all be arrested or shot on sight under the curfew. No curfew right now. So we're lucky."

"No curfew *yet*," Vox corrected him. "We nearly ended up dead in the sewers."

"I warned you about those sewers," the old man said. "You didn't listen."

"It was Plan B," Vox said. "His Majesty here ended up being more difficult than I thought."

"I warned you about that, too," the old man said.

Vox looked up at him, irritated. "Are you enjoying this?"

"People are dead," the old man said somberly. "There's nothing to enjoy about that." He paused and then added, "But, otherwise, yes. I do enjoy the opportunity to say I told you so."

"Soak it up," Vox said. "It's probably not going to happen again."

"Probably not," the old man agreed. He nodded at Nax. "Your Majesty. It's an honor to meet you."

"I wish I could say the same," Nax replied. "But since I don't know anyone's name, I can't say that I've met any of you."

"That's understandable." The old man didn't sound offended. "But as I'm sure Vox here has already explained to you, we can't risk being discovered by the authorities."

"Then perhaps you should reconsider your current course of action," Nax suggested. "Unless the law has changed since I've been gone, aiding and abetting a traitor carries the same penalty as treason does."

"Yes it does," the old man agreed.

"Then, if you don't mind me asking, what would prompt you to do this?"

The old man and the woman looked surprised. They turned to Vox, who shook his head.

"You didn't tell him?" the old man asked.

"And put all your lives at risk? Of course I didn't tell him."

"Our lives are at risk every day," the old man said.

"Every time we meet," the woman added.

"This is a different risk," Vox said.

"The punishment is still the same," the old man said.

Vox shook his head again. "I knew I should have kept you out of this."

The old man turned back to Nax and leaned forward, resting his elbows on the back of his legs. "You have no idea who we are?"

"Considering that Vox spent a great deal of time trying

to convince me that everyone on this planet wanted me dead-"

"Well, according to some polls it's only seventy-five percent," the woman interrupted. "And that's skewed. So maybe it's more, most likely it's less."

"And based on what Vox has told me about his mission," Nax continued, "and what I've already observed, my working theory is that you're some kind of political revolutionaries."

"Political revolutionaries," the woman echoed.

"Considering that none of you have tried to turn me in yet," Nax added.

The old man laughed. "That's pretty close."

Vox glared at the old man. "Don't do this."

The old man waved him off and held up his hand, his thumb, forefinger and index finger pressed together and upright in the standard Natuzzi greeting. "Your Majesty, it's a pleasure to meet you. I'm Pastor Cavon Tai of the Evangelical Church of Christ."

25

"THIS IS…INTERESTING," Hawkins said from the empty seat beside Nax.

Naturally, Nax didn't respond. He just sat there, staring at the old man, not saying anything.

"As I recall," Hawkins continued. "There's only one religion on Natuzzi? One government sanctioned religion. Anything else is considered, what's the word?" She snapped her fingers. *Heretical.*"

There was a bump as the vehicle rolled over something in the road and everyone jostled in their seats.

"Anyone caught practicing a religion outside of the Natuzzi government sanctioned religion is considered to be a traitor," Hawkins said. "Wow. When you think about it, you people have a lot of things that are considered treasonous. That's got to be a problem, right? I mean, you guys can't possibly function as a society when over half your rules are punishable by *death*."

Nax still didn't say anything.

Hawkins leaned forward, studying the old man. "Where would a Natuzzi even *hear* about Christianity? That sounds like the sort of thing the government would have a pretty tight lockdown on, doesn't it?" She glanced at Nax, as if expecting some kind of reaction. But there was none. However, her gaze did fall upon Vox. "Ah. Maybe your secret agent buddy is moonlighting as a missionary? Well, *hell*, that would be a twist." She sat back. "I can't remember, does the UPA sanction destabilizing governments through the use of outside religions? Blink once for yes, twice for no."

Nax didn't blink.

Hawkins shook her head. "No, I can't imagine Wana-maker sending an agent into deep undercover with a *Bible*. That doesn't sound like him. That sounds sloppy and Wana-maker isn't sloppy. At least, I didn't think he was. Of course, here we are, traveling with a bunch of people who are going to end up dead because they decided to turn their lives over to another god and stop believing the Natuzzi were the center of the universe." She took a breath and exhaled slowly. "That really puts it into perspective, don't you think?"

Nax didn't answer.

"Right," Hawkins said, as if he had. "Of course you would think that way. But, I did tell you not to trust him." She nodded at Vox. "And here you are, surrounded by a group of people who the government want dead just as much as they want you dead. Instead of a shield, you're dousing yourself with grade A plasma accelerant. You're all going to blow up *spectacularly*." She leaned in, resting her hand on his shoulder and whispered into his ear. "If you were smart, you'd jump out of this vehicle right now. Your chances of survival improve dramatically if you're not running with a crew of dead men."

Nax gently rolled his shoulders back, shrugging her hand off.

Hawkins sighed. "Don't say I didn't warn you."

26

AFTER IT BECAME clear that Nax wasn't going to say anything, Vox glared at Tai. "I warned you."

"Please, don't talk to me like I'm a child," Tai said. "If there is anyone in the Royal Family who would understand, it would be this man right now."

Vox pointed at him. "That's a mistake on your part. A mistake that could cost your life and everybody else's in this church."

"Stop being such an alarmist."

"I'm being *practical*."

Tai focused on Nax. "Your Majesty-"

"You should really stop calling me that," Nax said finally.

"Well, despite everything, your title hasn't been rescinded," Tai said. "You're still a member of the Royal Family."

"That doesn't mean you need to keep reminding me of it," Nax said.

Tai nodded. "That seems fair."

"How far out are we?" Vox asked the driver.

"Another twenty," the driver said. "Maybe longer. I'm getting reports of checkpoints going up."

Vox turned back to his scanner. "This is going bad faster than I would like."

"Is there an ideal speed for this going bad?" the woman asked.

"Yes, as slowly as possible." Vox rubbed the side of his head. "The narrative was supposed to be that Nax had been taken by Kel's group."

The woman tapped a finger against her lips thoughtfully. "I seem to recall there was somebody recently who talked about how the media has their own narrative these days."

"Stop it," Vox said.

Nax studied the old man carefully. "Your church is tantamount to high treason."

"I am aware of that," Tai said. "It's one of the things we're hoping to change."

"How do you plan on changing that?" Nax asked.

"One day at a time," Tai replied. "One person at a time."

"The government can wipe out your entire group at once," Nax said.

"Yes, that's been pointed out to me once or twice," Tai said.

"One person, one day at a time seems like a losing plan," Nax said.

"To be fair, though," Tai said, "there aren't a lot of options that would be considered a winning plan for us."

"Then why do this to yourselves?" Nax asked.

Tai shrugged. "You know anything about the story of Christ?"

"A thing or two," Nax said. "A fellow crew member on my ship counts himself among your...tribe."

The old man grinned. "Tribe. I like the sound of that." He looked at the woman. "That sounds good, doesn't it?"

She nodded. "It has a ring to it."

Vox looked up from his scanner. "Look, this is not the time for this."

"This is *exactly* the time for it," Tai replied.

"No, it's not," Vox said. "We've got incoming from all sides. We need to stay focused on the mission here."

"Right now, the mission here is getting the two of you from point A to point B," Tai said. "There's nothing else to do, so we might as well do this."

Nax turned to Vox. "Is this you?"

Vox looked at him with tense concern. "The next words out of your mouth better not be what I think they're going to be."

"I'm confused," the woman said, looking back and forth between Nax and Vox, before finally settling on Tai. "Is there something I'm missing?"

The old man shrugged. "If there is, I'm missing it, too."

"You need to remember the ramifications that we're looking at here," Vox said.

"I'm not the one who put you in this position," Nax replied.

"No, but you're starting to sound like the one who's going to make my position a lot worse."

"I was perfectly content staying in the palace," Nax said.

"Where you surely would have died," Tai said, jumping back in.

Nax looked down at his hands. "I had made my peace with that."

"Well, I'm sorry to hear that," Tai said softly.

The driver swore.

"What is it?' Vox asked.

The vehicle jolted to a stop.

"I just got the notification. There's a checkpoint on the Bonino Bridge," the driver said. "We won't make it across."

"Damnit," Vox muttered.

"We could take the Savio Ridgeway," the driver said.

"But that's going to take too long," Vox finished for him. "We don't have that kind of time."

"And how much time do we have?" Nax asked.

"Not enough," Vox said. "At this rate, even if we could make it across the Bonino Bridge, I'm worried somebody will have gotten wise and canceled your access to the Vault."

"So what do you want to do now?" Tai asked.

"We can't just give up and turn back," the woman said. "There's no place to go back to."

Vox rubbed his chin and sighed. "We're going to have to see if Kel and his Freedom Movement are willing to take us in for real."

27

USS DEFIANCE

"DOCTOR, HAVE A SEAT." Cooper gestured to the empty chair on the other side of the desk.

Doctor Marlize Dheer hesitated, her hand resting on the back of the chair. It was Mitchell's office, but the man sitting behind the desk was decidedly not the captain.

Cooper looked up from the screen he was reading when he realized she hadn't sat down. "You're confused."

"I wasn't aware we had a new first officer," Dheer said cautiously.

"Yes, I was a late addition," Cooper said. "Captain Mitchell didn't have the opportunity to introduce me to the crew before getting himself stuck on that comet." The last part was delivered with a strong dose of sarcasm.

Dheer still didn't sit down. She tapped her fingers against the back of the chair.

"If you're worried that I'm some kind of imposter," Cooper said. "I can show you my file."

"I'm not worried you're some kind of imposter," Dheer said. "If it was something like that, the crew would have already caught on."

"Oh?" Cooper raised an eyebrow. "Is that so?"

"Although, that's something a cocky imposter who's confident he's not going to get caught would say."

Cooper gestured at the chair again. "Please. Sit down, Doctor. I imagine this is going to be a lengthy conversation and it'll be more comfortable for you if you sit."

Dheer hesitated again, but then complied. "What can I do for you, Commander?"

Cooper turned back to his screen for a moment, reading the last few sentences before asking, "What's your opinion on Captain Mitchell's mental state."

Dheer managed to keep a neutral expression. "I beg your pardon?"

Cooper turned off his monitor and sat back in his chair, folding his hands together under his chin. "I'd like to hear your professional thoughts on the captain's mental wellbeing."

Dheer folded her hands in her lap. "I believe that's something best asked of Doctor Rabkin. After all, he is the ship's CMO."

Cooper nodded. "Yes, that's true. But Doctor Rabkin and Captain Mitchell have a long friendship, spanning decades. I'm looking for an opinion that's a little less biased."

"Biased?"

Cooper shifted in his seat. "Captain Mitchell has displayed...behaviors that I find to be concerning."

"Let me make sure I'm getting this straight," Dheer said. "You want me to tell you that the captain isn't fit for duty?"

"That's not what I said at all," Cooper said. "I said I wanted you to give me your professional opinion on his mental wellbeing."

"And what do you plan on doing with this medical opinion?"

"I plan on using it to inform any command decisions I may have to make since our captain finds himself stuck on a comet that's conveniently in Natuzzi space," Cooper said.

"Their situation doesn't sound particularly great, I'll grant you that."

Cooper nodded. "No, it does not."

"But that doesn't mean the captain isn't fit for duty."

"I never even suggested that he wasn't," Cooper said. "I simply wanted to hear your professional, medical opinion."

Dheer took a deep breath and met Cooper's gaze evenly. "Well, in my professional medical opinion, I believe that Captain Mitchell's mental health is fine. He hasn't exhibited any behaviors or mannerisms that I believe are cause for concern."

Copper nodded again. "Well, I suppose that's not a surprising assessment."

"That's good to hear."

"Now, how would you like to explain the captain's decision regarding Ensign Calloway?"

Dheer jerked her head slightly, caught off guard by the question. "I'm sorry, what?"

"Ensign Erin Calloway? She's currently in a coma in the medbay? She's been unresponsive for nearly three weeks?"

"I know who she is," Dheer said, snapping slightly. "I'm her attending physician."

"And why is that?"

"I don't follow."

"This ship is not equipped to handle a patient in a long-term coma," Cooper said.

"We don't know what the extent of her coma is."

"Has she displayed any indication in the last three weeks that she might wake up?"

"No."

"Then I think, perhaps, it's safe to say that she's in a long-term coma," Cooper said. "Or, at the very least, she's in a vegetative state that is beyond the resources of this ship to handle on an indefinite basis."

"Except that I am handling it."

"For now," Cooper said. "What happens when we find ourselves in a position where we need that room for a patient who's not in a vegetative state?"

"What exactly are you suggesting?" Dheer asked, getting defensive.

"I'm asking why hasn't the captain transferred Ensign Calloway into the care of at least the *Atlantic*? They would be able to maintain her condition without it being a drain on their resources."

"Ensign Calloway is *not* a drain on our resources," Dheer said.

Cooper gestured to the monitor he had been reading on. "I just finished reading department and system reports for the last week. Ensign Calloway is not only using nearly two hundred kilowatts of power having that equipment monitor her on a daily basis, but the medbay only has four private rooms. With Ensign Calloway currently occupying one of those rooms indefinitely, that leaves you with only three, and on average, according to your medical reports, those three rooms are occupied for approximately four hours of every day."

"That leaves twenty other hours in the day where the other rooms are unoccupied," Dheer replied. "So I guess what I'm trying to say is: I don't see your point."

"My point is Ensign Calloway shouldn't be on this ship," Cooper said. "You're not a medical vessel and you don't have any medical staff trained for maintaining patients in long-term vegetative states."

"It's a coma," Dheer replied. "The computer does most of the work and even if it didn't, the condition is pretty low maintenance. She's basically asleep."

"And what happens when the ship is under attack?" Cooper asked.

"The same thing that happens every time: the shit hits the fan."

Cooper frowned. "You're purposely being difficult, Doctor."

"No," she said. "It just comes naturally to me. Ensign Calloway is a member of this crew, if Captain Mitchell wants to keep her in our care, that's certainly his prerogative. There's nothing in the Fleet code that says he's breaking any rules."

"True." Cooper said it slowly, as if he was buying a few seconds to come up with another tactic. "But there's an argument to be made that he's being irresponsible with Ensign Calloway's quality of life."

Dheer shrugged. "Maybe. I don't see it as a hill that anybody would want to die on."

"Die, no," Cooper said. "But it's a good place to start making a stand."

Dheer frowned. "This sounds like you're looking for a reason to remove Captain Mitchell from active duty."

"I don't have to look for a reason, Doctor," Cooper said. "The captain's likely to do it to himself. What are the odds he's coming back from that comet?"

"I wasn't aware we were concerned that his return wasn't a forgone conclusion."

Cooper leaned forward, resting his arms on the table. "I'm not a fool, Doctor. I know that Captain Mitchell is up to something regarding Lieutenant Commander Nax. I can read the writing on the wall. It's out of respect for this crew that I haven't reached out to the admiralty yet."

Dheer folded her arms. "And what would you even say to the admiralty?"

"That the captain is on the verge of inciting a conflict with one of the UPA's most valued members."

Dheer scoffed at that. "Nobody considers Natuzzi to be of any value."

"I can forward along some relevant reading material," Cooper said. "The D'Ambra administration is extremely motivated to get the Natuzzi more involved with the UPA as a whole."

"That doesn't make them valuable."

"As a matter of fact, that's exactly what it does."

Dheer shook her head. "Fine. Whatever. I don't particularly care one way or another. There's a reason I became a doctor and not a politician."

"Then you'll have to trust me when I say that the captain is one transmission away from being stripped of his rank and kicked out of the Fleet altogether."

Dheer got to her feet. "I'm not comfortable with the direction of this conversation."

"That's understandable."

"Because it sounds like you're suggesting a mutiny."

Cooper rolled his eyes. "Please. Don't be so dramatic. And besides, it's not mutiny if it's a direct order from the admiralty."

"Doesn't make it right."

"Actually, it does."

"'I was just following orders?'"

Cooper sighed. "I didn't call you here to pick a fight with

you, Doctor. If I wanted that, I would have brought in Rabkin."

She held up her hands. "Then why am I here?"

"For exactly the reason I told you: I want to get your professional, unbiased opinion on Captain Mitchell's mental wellbeing."

Dheer didn't answer for a moment. She just stared at him, trying to get some kind of measure of who he was and not liking any of the measurements she was coming up with.

"In my professional, unbiased medical opinion, Captain Gavin Mitchell is of sound mind and being. He has full control over all his mental faculties and hasn't displayed any questionable lapses in judgment."

Cooper leaned back in his chair and spread out his hands. "Well, there you go, then."

"Is there anything else I can help you with?"

"Yes, actually, there is one other thing. I understand you put in a request for a transfer a month or so back."

Dheer paused. "I withdrew that request."

"Yes, I'm aware of that."

"How exactly did you find out about it, then?"

"The system still logs the request, even if it's not passed up through the chain of command."

"That means you would have had to go looking for it."

"That's exactly what I did," Cooper said.

"That seems like an unnecessary effort to make for something that didn't happen," Dheer said cautiously.

"I like to know as much as I can about the crew that I'm joining," Cooper said. "I did a deep dive on every member of *Defiance*'s command staff."

"Looking for canceled transfer requests?"

"Among other things."

"Like what?"

He gave her a dismissive wave. "Nothing that's relevant to our conversation. Right now I'm more interested in why you wanted to leave."

"I had some concerns about how Doctor Rabkin was running his staff."

"What kind of concerns?"

Dheer shrugged. "Rabkin has an abrasive command style. It takes some getting used to."

"That doesn't really answer the question."

"It's not really an issue anymore," she said.

"But it was."

"And then it wasn't."

"You canceled the request."

"Rabkin and I had a conversation," she said.

"About?"

Dheer shrugged again. "I don't quite recall the specifics."

"How about the broad strokes of it?"

She pressed her lips together tightly. "I called him out on his bullshit."

Cooper raised his eyebrows in surprise. "And how did that go?"

"Well, I canceled my request," she said. "So it must have gone pretty well. Why are you bringing this up?"

"Just trying to get a better understanding of the crew dynamics," he explained. "How are you feeling about your post now?"

"I'm very content where I am."

Cooper nodded. "Content. That's good."

"I'm glad you approve. Is there anything else I can help you with?"

He shook his head. "That's all for now."

"It was a pleasure to meet you," Dheer said, with a distinct lack of pleasure in her voice.

Cooper gave her a small nod. "Likewise."

She turned and left the office without another word.

Cooper turned his monitor back on and went back to reviewing all the available mission logs that he had access to.

28

NATUZZI SCOUT VESSEL

"THIS IS GOING to end very badly," Keane said, settling into the pilot's chair.

Mitchell leaned over his shoulder, looking out the viewscreen of the small vessel. "You're worried about what happens when we run into a border patrol?"

Keane made a noise from the back of his throat. He flipped some switches to his left and adjusted the output of the screen immediately in front of him. "Oh, things are going to end badly long before that." He pointed at the haphazard labels that were all over the console. "These read like half-assed translations."

Mitchell picked up one of the labels. "That's probably because they are."

"Wanamaker couldn't be bothered to get somebody out here who could actually read Natuzzi?" Keane activated what he thought were the main thrusters. He heard a low thrumming sound from the rear of the ship.

"To be fair, there was only one person who had to be able to read these." Mitchell put the label back and looked for another seat to settle into.

The scout ship was a little smaller than a standard Fleet shuttle and the cockpit made it feel even smaller. It was clearly built to handle no more than two crew members at a time, but anything more than one was obviously going to be uncomfortable.

Mitchell found a second seat squeezed between a console and an empty storage container. "Are you going to be able to fly it?"

"Do I have the option to say no?"

"Not really."

Keane made a few more adjustments and the overhead lights dimmed to the point of near darkness. "Okay, I don't think I'm supposed to do that."

"That doesn't sound very reassuring," Mitchell said.

"Well, captain, if it helps I'm not feeling very reassured myself." Keane grabbed one of the labels and flipped it upside down. "I think that makes more sense?" He adjusted something else and the lights went back to full. "Hey, there's that."

"Great. So we don't have to make the trip in near darkness," Mitchell said. "Things are finally looking up."

Keane glanced back at him. "Anybody ever tell you you're not that funny?"

"No," Mitchell said. "Probably because they're concerned that it'd be a court-martial offense."

Keane turned back to the controls. "That's a pretty good point there."

"I thought so." Mitchell adjusted the straps on his seat. "How long till we get to Natuzzi?"

"According to flight logs on file, it's a two-hour trip," Keane said. "Though, I'd rather not do anything that's going to catch anybody's attention."

"And I'd rather not spend any more time than necessary on the wrong side of this border," Mitchell replied.

"Amen to that." Keane fired the maneuvering thrusters until they were out of range of the Ahines' comet. Then he fired up the main engine and everything in the cockpit rattled. "Wow and I thought the *Defiance* was on shaky ground."

"The *Defiance* has the good fortune to be under the care of Jaxson Warrick," Mitchell said. "I'm afraid what we might find if we look into the service logs for this ship."

"You think there's actually a service log on file?" Keane asked in disbelief.

"I'm afraid that there isn't."

Keane increased their speed and looked for something that resembled an autopilot function. "Can I ask you a question, Captain?"

"Is it about why the *Defiance* hasn't actually fallen apart yet?"

"It's about why you felt okay with the notion of leaving Cooper unsupervised."

"Commander Cooper doesn't need supervision," Mitchell said. "According to his file, he's a fine officer, with several letters of commendation and multiple honors awarded to him."

"But he's not a member of Directive Fifty-Two."

Mitchell watched the stars pass them by as the ship increased speed. "No, he is not."

Keane glanced back at him. "You see where I'm going with this?"

"The thought has certainly crossed my mind," Mitchell said.

"Is there a particular reason Sadie wasn't given the

promotion?" Keane asked. "That is, if you don't mind me asking."

"A little late to ask if I mind."

Keane just shrugged.

"The reason, beyond the fact that Sadler didn't want it, was the fact that it was out of my hands."

"Out of your hands?"

"Cooper was assigned by the admiralty, under a recommendation from the President himself."

"Well, shit," Keane said.

"Yeah. Pretty much."

"And you still think it was a good idea to leave him unsupervised on the ship?"

"What do you suggest, Keane?" Mitchell asked. "He's not a child."

"Well, yeah, no."

"The man is still an officer in good standing with the Fleet," Mitchell said. "I can't just treat him like a spy the moment he came on board."

"Well, you could," Keane said. "It would just be awkward if it turned out he was legitimately just here to be your XO without any kind of secret agenda."

"Do you think it was an accident that I 'forgot' about him before we left the *Atlantic*?"

"Admittedly, it did seem a little out of character for you, Captain."

"It's not ideal," Mitchell said. "But you need to have a little faith in the crew."

"Ah. Right, *faith*. Sure," Keane said with the kind of tone one uses to placate a family member who refuses to accept the obvious.

"Got something specific on your mind you want to share, Commander?" Mitchell asked.

Keane shook his head. "Not particularly. Just, you know, trying to get a handle on what's going on around here."

Mitchell settled back in his seat. "It is what it is."

"And what is it, then?" Keane asked. "Because right now, it feels like I should be worried about whether or not Cooper's going to have an armed escort waiting for you when we get back."

"Do you really think Rabkin would let him get away with that?" Mitchell asked.

"First, Rabkin's what, ninety years old? He's not going to be standing in anybody's way. Second, it's not a matter of letting anybody get away with anything," Keane said. "Cooper would have regulations on his side. It would be easy enough to present a case to the crew that you're not fit for duty."

Mitchell gave him a bemused look. "Something you've been considering lately?"

"Just trying to stay on top of all the possible scenarios," Keane said. "Hell, I've got plans to take down Zemble, if need be."

"I didn't realize your trust issues with the crew ran so deep," Mitchell said.

"It pays to have contingency plans in place."

"And what contingency plans do you have in place for me being declared unfit for duty?"

"Depends on who's doing the declaring," Keane said.

"If it's you?"

Keane looked back at him. "Do you really want to know the answer to that?"

Mitchell frowned. "No, not really."

Keane turned back to the controls. "Didn't think so."

"What's your contingency for Cooper having taken command when we get back?"

"*If* we get back." Keane tapped a monitor on his left. "This is a livestream of Natuzzi Fleet positions."

"Good thing to have if you're trying to fly through their space undetected."

"Looks like they're redeploying about half their fleet."

Mitchell leaned forward in surprise. "*Half* their fleet? Where?"

"The Veneer border."

29

NATUZZI

"HOW MANY OF YOU ARE THERE?" Nax asked.

Tai seemed confused by the question at first. Apart from the driver they were alone. Vox and the woman had exited the transport and disappeared after they had parked behind a nondescript domicile.

Nax sat away from the window, but angled himself so he could still get a view of anyone approaching their transport. Outside, the amber sky was slowly darkening as the Natuzzi sun began its descent. He tried to remember the last time he had seen a Natuzzi sunset and found that he couldn't.

After a few seconds, Tai realized what Nax was talking about. "You mean members of the church."

Nax nodded.

"Well, as I'm sure you can understand, we try not to document too much about the church," Tai said. "Anything written down can be found by the wrong people."

"It could also be found by the right people," the driver said.

Nax glanced up at the driver and then back at Tai.

"It's a minor point of contention," Tai said. "Much of what we have is passed around orally, person to person. We like to limit recordings as much as possible."

"Puts too much emphasis on trying to memorize things," the driver said.

"It's not a bad thing," Tai countered. "Memorizing scripture can come in handy when you're facing times of trials and tribulations."

"Doesn't make it any easier to have to memorize it," the driver said.

Tai chuckled softly. "Your question was how many of us are there?"

Nax nodded again. "I was beginning to worry you might have forgotten."

"Well, in our little cell, there's six," Tai said. "Me." He gestured to the driver. "Gil. Sha is the lovely lady that you met with Vox."

"Who's not going to be happy that you're giving him all of our names," Gil interrupted him.

"We all have names for a reason," Tai said. "Which is so that we know who we're talking about without having to go through elaborate descriptions of people."

"I'm the Driver. How is that elaborate?"

Tai ignored him. "There are, of course, three others in our cell and as a compromise, I won't share their names with you."

"Vox isn't one of them?"

Tai shook his head. "No. Vox is...a friend."

Nax frowned. "What kind of friend?"

"The non-believing kind, unfortunately," Tai said. "I've tried to talk with him about it, but he's made it very clear he's not interested."

"Can you afford to have that kind of friend right now?" Nax asked.

"He may not share our spiritual beliefs, but we all share the same secular beliefs."

"Which are?"

"All Natuzzi are created equal," Tai said. "And no Natuzzi should be punished for believing in something that's not sanctioned by the government."

Nax glanced back out the window, but there was no sign of Vox or Sha. "So there's six in your church?"

"There's six in most churches," Tai said. "We like to keep the number low. Low numbers are less likely to set off any alarms. Did you know that any gathering over thirty needs to be registered with the local Community Director?"

"I vaguely recall that," Nax replied.

"Failure to do so, of course, can result in fines or jail time," Gil added.

"So, as I'm sure you understand, six is a good number to keep individual churches at," Tai said.

"Sound advice," Nax agreed. "How many churches are there?"

"Last I heard, there were three others in this community alone," Tai said. "Across the province, though, there's less than thirty. Beyond that...?" He shrugged. "I couldn't tell you. It's dangerous to reach out too far."

"You want to give him addresses while you're at it?" Gil asked.

Tai waved a dismissive hand at him. "Stop it."

"If he gets caught..."

"They'll probably shoot him on sight." Tai paused and regarded Nax with a sympathetic look. "Apologies. But-"

"It's true," Nax agreed.

Tai nodded.

"So you don't have any communication with the other churches?"

"We do," Tai said. "It's just very contained and limited. Members closest to the province borders are usually tasked with reaching out. They're the ones most likely to have business, professional or personal, in the neighboring province, so it stands to reason they would be the ones who would garner the least amount of suspicion."

"This is a dangerous path you've set yourself down," Nax said.

"Dangerous, but also rewarding."

"You find the prospect of dying, branded as a traitor rewarding?"

"I find the prospect of eternal life with our Creator far more rewarding than spending eternity in the burning pits of Hell," Tai replied. "This isn't what you expected to find when you came back here, is it?"

"In all fairness," Nax said. "I never actually expected to come back."

Tai nodded. "I can certainly appreciate that."

"How did this happen?"

"How did what happen?"

Nax leaned forward. "Who brought *this* to Natuzzi?"

"Ah. Who brought the Word of God to Natuzzi?"

"Sure. Let's put it that way."

Tai didn't answer for a moment. "If you don't mind me asking, and you'll have to forgive me if I'm stepping over any lines here. But you have to understand that despite everything, you're still a member of the Royal Family and outside of this current situation, there was no way I was ever going to be speaking with you or any member of your family."

"I'm no different than you are."

Tai held out his hand and then turned it over. "Well, I don't think that's entirely true. You've spent quite a bit of time off-planet. In fact, I believe I heard one report suggest that you might have even set a record. No other Natuzzi has been off-planet as long as you have."

"And has come back alive," Gil added.

"I'm sure they'll make a point of that during my execution," Nax replied dryly.

Tai chuckled softly again and then held up an apologetic hand. "I'm sorry. I shouldn't be laughing."

"I'll let you know if you step over any lines," Nax said.

"Fair enough, I suppose," Tai replied. He took a moment to compose himself. "After all your time off-planet, do you still find yourself clinging to the tenets of the Natuzzi belief system?"

"It's not something I've given much thought to," Nax replied.

Tai studied him for a long moment and then frowned disapprovingly. "Well, we both know that's a lie."

"There," Nax said.

"What?"

"That's a line you just stepped over."

Tai raised his hand and pointed at Nax, but didn't say anything. After a moment, he lowered his hand and turned to stare out the window. "To answer your question, I don't really know."

"It wasn't Vox?"

Tai turned back to him in surprise. "Vox? No. The church has been here longer than any of us have been alive."

"That's not possible."

Tai shrugged. "And yet it is."

"Where did it come from?"

"Well, I suppose the correct answer is God," Tai said. "But that's not the answer you're looking for."

"There hasn't been a secondary system of belief in over a thousand years," Nax said.

"And where did you learn that?"

"The same place everybody learns it," Nax replied. "The history books."

"And who writes the history books?" Tai asked.

Nax took a moment to absorb this. "What you're suggesting..."

"Shouldn't be all that surprising," Tai said. "Not after what you've experienced in the last few days."

Nax didn't say anything.

"The truth is never convenient," Tai said.

There was a knock at the rear door before it opened. Vox and Sha stood there. Vox gestured at Nax. "Come on. I got us a meeting."

Tai started to get up with Nax but Vox stopped him. "No," he said. "You're going home."

"Home?" Tai echoed.

Vox looked pointedly at Tai, Gil and Sha. "All three of you."

"Oh, come on," Sha started to say.

Vox shook his head. "It's not up for discussion. Go home and forget about any of this. There's nothing else you can help with."

Gil started up the transport. "Sounds like a good idea to me."

"We'll leave you here," Tai said. "But I disagree that there's nothing more we can do." He helped Sha back into the transport.

"Anything you do from this point on will put you right in the line of fire," Vox warned. "Don't do that to yourselves."

"Don't worry," Tai assured him. "I promise you, we'll be certain not to do anything outside the anonymity provided to us from the privacy of our homes."

Nax looked at him. "And what assistance do you think you'll be able to provide from the safety of your homes?"

Tai smiled warmly. "Why, prayer, of course."

30

"THEY DON'T KNOW," Nax said. "Do they?"

"Know what?" Vox asked.

They made their way through the back rooms of a large industrial building. Nax didn't recognize the logo on the outside, but he knew a mineral processing plant when he saw one.

"They don't know that you're not...a *local*," Nax said.

Vox stopped abruptly and turned back to face him. "Did you tell them?"

"It didn't seem like the prudent play to make," Nax replied. "But the thought did cross my mind."

Vox grumbled something under his breath that Nax couldn't make out and started walking again.

"How exactly would it benefit you to align yourself with a group that would almost certainly be executed the moment they were discovered?" Nax asked.

"It's complicated."

"What do you think their reaction would be?" Nax asked. "They seem to regard you as a valued ally."

Vox didn't respond.

"How did you even find them?" Nax asked.

"I didn't. They found me."

"Then that raises more questions."

"I'm sure it does," Vox said. "But I'm not going to be able to answer any of them for you."

"You're not the one who brought the church here, are you?"

Vox looked back at him in confusion. "What?"

"Tai explained to me that the church has been here for quite some time," Nax continued. "But this is a concept I'm having difficulty accepting."

"And it's less difficult to think I'm the one who contaminated your people?"

"I didn't say that."

"No, but you were thinking it." Vox took them around a corner and up a series of glass-enclosed stairs. "I didn't bring anything here. Whatever's going on with these churches, it has nothing to do with me."

"Although you haven't hesitated to take advantage of it."

"I'm hardly taking advantage of them," Vox said.

"What services do you provide them?" Nax asked.

"I help pass along intel," Vox replied.

"Intel that you conveniently get to look at first."

"I never promised anyone that I wouldn't."

"Which then begs the question: What are you doing here?"

"I thought that was pretty clear," Vox replied. "I'm trying to get access to the Sicurezza Vault."

Nax grabbed his shoulder and brought him to a stop. "What are you doing *here*? On *Natuzzi*?" He locked eyes with Vox and lowered his voice to a whisper. "What's your primary mission objective?"

"I can't tell you that."

"Can't or won't?"

"Not much of a difference between the two right now." Vox shrugged off his hand. "Come on, the clock is still ticking."

They reached the top of the stairs where a clear glass-enclosed platform gave Nax a perfect view of the mineral processing equipment below.

"Something doesn't add up," Nax continued. "An op like this would have been set up long before the Veneer Empire collapsed. The resources needed to just...*prepare* you would have taken at least twelve months. You're not here because of the Natuzzi interest in Veneer space. At least, not initially."

"If you're looking to get both of us killed before we leave this place, by all means, please keep it up," Vox hissed back at him.

"You didn't bring the churches here," Nax continued, careful to keep his voice lower. "The Natuzzi interest in the Veneer Empire appears to be a secondary objective. So what was your primary objective?"

Vox didn't answer. They reached the end of the platform. Before opening the door, he took a deep breath and then turned to Nax.

"I want you to understand what we're doing here."

"I'm eager to have that understanding as well," Nax replied.

"This is not an ideal solution," Vox continued. "I don't even know that I would call it the lesser of two evils. But right now it's the only option we have. There's a very real possibility that neither one of us is going to walk out of here alive."

"That seems to defeat the purpose of all this," Nax replied.

"Yeah, it's not something I'm happy with either," Vox said.

"As I recall, you told me with some pride that you have excellent improvisational skills," Nax said. "This particular move would suggest otherwise."

"There's a sweet spot with somebody like Dalin Kel," Vox said.

Nax arched one of his hairless eyebrows. "A sweet spot?"

"He's a bit power hungry," Vox explained. "That part is fairly obvious to anyone."

"It's an assumption I certainly made and I haven't even had the pleasure of meeting him."

"He can be prone to making rapid, sometimes overly harsh decisions about things," Vox continued.

"You seem to be suggesting that he's unstable," Nax said.

"Well, one of the reasons the Queen has delayed any serious response is the fact that Dalin Kel suffers from Fey's Euphoria."

31

"I CERTAINLY DID NOT SEE *this* coming," Hawkins whispered into Nax's ear. "Did you? No, of course you didn't. And why should you? You're doing the best you can to ignore your condition. Why would it ever occur to you that you might encounter somebody who has the same condition? Who was the last person you saw that had Fey's? Before you left? The man in that village? The one who lived in that small shack by the water?"

"Stop it," Nax whispered.

Vox looked back at him. "What?"

Nax shook his head. "Nothing."

They stepped through the doorway into a large meeting room with a dozen or so Natuzzi dressed in black uniforms. The room had a ramshackle, hurriedly set up appearance to it. Monitors and consoles sat on desks and hard wires ran into walls. The room hummed with activity; but that hum came to a stop as soon as Nax entered.

"Is it me?" Hawkins asked. "You think they can see me?"

"When they told me you wanted to meet with me, I thought they were mistaken," said a raspy voice from the shadows at the back of the room. "Or worse, perhaps. The wayward prince himself seeking an audience with *me*? No, no, no. That's not how these things are done. And, after all, you had far bigger things on your mind than meeting with me. But, yet, here you are." The man in the shadows coughed. "Here you are."

Vox stepped forward, positioning himself between Nax and everyone else. "Let's all remember, we were expected. *Invited.*"

"You invited yourselves," replied the raspy voice. "That hardly counts."

"You could have said no," Vox said.

"I could have," the man agreed. He stepped forward out of the shadows, hobbling a little as he walked. He grabbed a nearby table for support. His skin was a burnt shade of orange and there were a collection of scars crisscrossing the left side of his face. He didn't seem any older than Tai had been, but the way he carried himself suggested that he was easily a decade older, if not more. His eyes were narrow and sharp; they looked past Vox and focused on Nax. "But for some reason, I'm already being blamed for taking the wayward prince. So it seemed pointless to say no." He squinted at Nax. "Are you real?"

"Well, that really cuts to the heart of the matter, doesn't it?" Hawkins asked.

He gestured to the people surrounding him. "If I asked them, would they all give me the same description of you? Would they simply humor me? Ask guiding questions in which I give them the answers they need to give to me?" He reached with an unsteady outstretched hand. "If I touched you now, would I feel you? Or would my mind convince me that I felt you, even though there was nothing to feel?"

"I don't think any answers I give are going to bring you any peace of mind one way or another," Nax said.

The man nodded. "Yes. That's true, I suppose." He stepped away from the table and raised his right hand, his index finger and middle finger pressed together and his ring finger and little finger lowered, and his thumb set apart. He bowed slightly at the waist. "Your Majesty, as I'm sure you're already aware, I am Dalin Kel. It's a pleasure to make your acquaintance."

Nax returned the gesture. "Good tidings."

Kel shook his fingers side-to-side. "Please, don't."

Nax looked at Kel and then Vox, confused. "Did I do something wrong?"

"While there are parts of our current system that I don't agree with," Kel said, "I still have the utmost respect for your position. And I'd rather you not lower yourself to my level."

"My position?" Nax repeated. "I'm currently wanted for treason and, as I understand it, accused of murder."

"Yes, yes," Kel said. "I've heard some truly terrible things about you recently. Although, I'm of the mind that one shouldn't believe everything they hear on the news. Besides, it's treason against a corrupt and flawed system." He gestured for them to sit down at an empty table. "As far as I'm concerned, you should be a hero of the people."

"And what about the part where I'm an alleged murderer?" Nax asked, taking a seat.

Kel shrugged, wincing as he sat down. "No one is perfect. I've done things I'm not proud of as well."

"So I've heard," Nax replied.

Kel glanced at Vox, a ghost of a smile passing across his face. "I'm sure you have." He made a gesture and a moment later someone arrived with a tray. On it was a small pitcher of purple liquid and three glasses. "I'm assuming it's been some time since you've had a glass of yasha?"

Nax looked at the pitcher with a mixture of surprise and regret. "It's not something...easily acquired outside of Natuzzi."

"I would imagine not." Kel poured them each a quarter of a glass. "I've heard rumors that there's nothing that compares to it out there."

Nax took the proffered glass and closed his eyes as he inhaled the sweet aroma. "No, not at all."

"How long then, has it been for you?" Kel asked.

"Over fifteen years," Nax replied, setting the glass back down without sampling the drink.

"That's a long time. Are you afraid you've lost the taste for it?"

"Not at all. I'm just painfully aware that this could be my last glass of yasha forever," Nax said. "I would like to let the moment last for as long as possible."

Kel smiled. "I appreciate a man who appreciates life. But," he gestured to the pitcher that was still over half full, "I have plenty left and I would hate for it to go to waste. So please, enjoy yourself."

Nax looked at the glass of yasha and hesitated again.

Hawkins was in the seat across from him, leaning across the table for a closer look at the purple liquid. "I don't get it. What is it? Is it alcohol?" She reached for the glass, but Nax grabbed it first.

He brought it to his lips and took a small sip. His eyes closed again as the liquid made its way across his tongue and down his throat, sending tiny sparkles of ecstasy through his taste buds. A tingling sensation traveled from there throughout his body, reaching the tips of his fingers before dissipating.

Hawkins slumped back in her seat, her eyes wide. "Wow."

Nax took a deep breath and set the glass back down without another sip.

"That's a hell of a thing," she breathed.

"Thank you," Nax said.

Kel tilted his head forward. "It truly is the simple things." He picked up his own glass and knocked back the entirety of its contents in a single gulp. He tossed the empty glass off to the side and it shattered as it struck the ground. He looked at the untouched glass in front of Vox. "Not thirsty, my friend?"

"What happens if a human drinks this?" Hawkins asked. "Is it the same kind of reaction? Is it worse? Do you even know?"

Nax avoided looking at her.

Kel pointed at Vox. "I would like to point out that in not partaking, you run the risk of offending me and if you're here for a favor, I don't think you want to do that."

Vox carefully pushed the glass back towards the center of the table. "It's a risk I'm willing to take."

Hawkins shivered. "Oooh, that's not going to end well, is it?"

"Well then." Kel nodded, seemingly unfazed, and folded his hands on the table. He turned back to Nax. "Did you know that up until only five hundred years ago, yasha was used for medicinal purposes only?"

Nax glanced at the pitcher between them. "I was not aware of that."

"Most aren't," Kel continued. "Prior to becoming what is considered to be the finest beverage this side of the Dorialen Belt, it was singularly used as a medication among patients suffering what at the time was considered a relatively minor ailment. Its original name escapes me, but these days you would be more familiar with its more conventionally known moniker: Fey's Euphoria."

Vox grumbled something under his breath. "Look, the history lesson is-"

Kel raised his hand sharply, silencing Vox with a look. "I'm not interested in whatever you have to say. At least, not right now. It's not often one has the good fortune to have an unsupervised audience with a member of the ruling family and I am determined to take full advantage of this opportunity."

"I'm hardly a member in good standing," Nax reminded him.

"And I myself have something of a checkered history with the public at large," Kel said. "So, therefore, I don't see how this simply isn't the perfect meeting." He lowered his hand back to the table. He looked momentarily confused. "Now, where was I?"

"Fey's Euphoria," Nax prompted, ignoring the look from Vox.

"Ah. Yes." Kel paused for a moment, collecting his thoughts. "Five hundred years ago, give or take a few years, Fey's Euphoria, then, of course, called something else entirely. It was a scientific name. Something long, complicated." He shook his head. "My apologies, I find myself easily distracted by the most mundane things. My point, as it was, is that Fey's Euphoria was, at best, a minor affliction affecting less than one percent of our population. It was routinely treated with a yasha solution, which seemed to curb the symptoms and, over time, resulted in an overall regression of the ailment." Kel clasped his hands together and grinned. "Yes, that's right. I can see the wheels turning, Your Majesty. What I am suggesting is that approximately five hundred years ago, give or take, we had what appears to be a cure for a disease that seems all but incurable today."

Nax took a slow, deep breath. "That's..."

"Difficult to believe." Kel nodded. "Yes, of course. Naturally, it is. Documentation from five hundred years ago, give or take, is not the easiest to come by and what one does find is not necessarily always the most reliable."

"And yet you seem to feel confident in your conclusions," Nax said.

"Confident," Kel murmured. "Confidence is a funny thing." He picked at something beneath his nails. "They say I have it, you know. Of course you do." He glanced briefly at Vox. "He would have told you. That's not an accusation, it's simply a fact."

"You say it like you don't believe it," Nax said.

"Well, facts are a funny thing as well," Kel said. "They seem to have a...malleable state to them, even when one is not confronted with having to question the very nature of reality." He raised a finger and gently shook it at Nax. "You're wondering about the yasha drink? It's one of the most popular beverages among our people. Statistically, it's consumed by at least one individual in every household and so the question on your mind is, if yasha was used to treat Fey's Euphoria five hundred years ago, give or take, and was doing it with what would be considered successful results, why is this a disease that plagues nearly *half* of our population?"

"Sure." Nax could feel Hawkins smirking inscrutably at him. "It's passed through my mind."

"Passed through your mind." Kel nodded. "Yes, well. Does the name Ireri Kio mean anything to you? You needn't bother answering, I already know the answer. No one familiar with this individual, despite the fact that he apparently, singlehandedly, changed the very nature of our species.

"You see, in its original form, the yashanive bean, from which yasha is derived, is quite *potent*. It has an intense bitterness that all but overwhelms the underlying sweetness." Kel paused. "I speak of these things as if that is how they are today, but thanks to the efforts of Ireri Kio, a biochemist who at the time was working for the Storemvile company, that is no longer the case." Kel reached forward and picked up the pitcher, pouring himself another glass. "He discovered that by manipulating the genetic makeup of the yashanive bean, specifically adding two DNA strands from the beetlebridge root, you can *remove* the bitterness of the yashanive bean altogether."

Kel took a sip from his new glass and reveled in the sweet aftertaste.

"The specifics, of course, escape us," he continued. "Five hundred years, give or take. Or, perhaps, it has less to do with simply time and more to do with *people*. Ireri Kio created a version of the yashanive bean that would create the most popular drink in our people's history and shortly afterwards, a minor ailment became a global epidemic."

Nax looked down at his own empty glass.

"Of course, now you are wondering why do we simply not use the unaltered yashanive bean? Surely it should still have some positive effect on those afflicted with Fey's. Well, therein lies the problem. The original yashanive bean no longer exists," Kel said. "It no longer grows anywhere on our planet or in our system. It is, effectively, extinct."

Nax slowly pushed his glass away. "That seems..."

"Suspicious," Kel said. "Yes, I agree. Do you know who founded Storemvile?" This time he didn't answer right away. He waited.

A momentary look of recognition passed through Nax's eyes, but he shook his head. "I can't recall."

"But you almost did," Kel said. "Yes?"

"There's something familiar about it, yes," Nax agreed.

"Gane Ngi," Kel said. "I'm sure it's a name you are very familiar with."

"The Ngi's became the ruling family in the late Bestion Century," Nax said.

"Nearly eighty years, give or take," Kel said, "after the events that I have just described to you. And during their time of power, Fey's Euphoria became the crippling epidemic it is today. Yes, I think suspicious is certainly the word I would use."

Nax remained composed as he met Kel's gaze. "I fail to see the relevancy of this history lesson."

Hawkins made a scoffing noise under her breath.

Kel raised his brow in mild surprise. "Oh?" He leaned forward. "They say I have the disease."

"You don't believe them," Nax said.

"Well, I question the authenticity of their statements," Kel said. "After all, how do I know what they're saying is real and not, well, a figment of my diseased mind?"

"Either way," Nax replied. "It doesn't bode well for you."

Kel leaned back in his seat. "No, I suppose it doesn't." He paused for a moment, his left hand moving in idle circles along the surface of the table. "Do you know there hasn't been a member of the Royal Family diagnosed with Fey's Euphoria in nearly a hundred years?"

"No, I did not know that," Nax replied.

"Statistically, they tell me, that is impossible."

"And yet..." Nax trailed off.

Kel nodded. "And yet," he agreed. He adjusted himself,

shifting his weight in the seat. "The Queen has steadfastly refused any requests to meet with me."

"So I've heard."

"It's been suggested to me that her hesitancy comes from my diagnosis," Kel said.

"Fey's is not contagious," Nax said.

"No, of course, it isn't," Kel agreed. "I believe the opinion is that it isn't so much a *physical* problem as it is a *political* problem. Meeting with a member of the opposition who is afflicted with our most popular disease...Well, it's been suggested to me that it lends an air of respectability to proceedings that the powers-that-be would rather be kept as...Well, they would just rather nobody think of it at all, really." He shrugged. "Personally, I believe your mother is concerned that she won't be able to keep up with me."

"It's certainly one point of view," Nax replied, attempting to sound as neutral as possible.

Kel grinned again. "Yes. A point of view. Why are you here, Your Majesty?"

Nax turned to Vox, but Kel shook his head.

"No, I don't want to hear from *him*," Kel said. "I have heard enough from him. I want to hear from *you*."

"I am not entirely certain why I am here," Nax said.

"No, you're not," Kel replied and, for the briefest of moments, his gaze moved to the seat where Hawkins sat. His pupils focused on her and his gaze narrowed, as if taking stock of an individual who hadn't previously been noticed.

Hawkins gasped, locking eyes with Kel.

Nax tensed, but didn't say anything.

But it was simply a moment. A second. Less than a second.

Kel blinked and turned to Vox. "Why are you here?"

Hawkins breathed a sigh of relief. "Well, *hell*."

Nax flinched slightly, but otherwise didn't move.

Kel pointed at Nax. "You're the most wanted man on our planet right now and you chose to come *here*, to see *me*. Surely you can see why I find such a thing to be...questionable." He coughed. "Depending on who you ask, I'm either the first or second most notorious member of our current political system. For all you know, I might be inclined to turn you back over to your mother."

"Except you haven't," Nax replied.

"I haven't *yet*," Kel corrected him. "I may not be young anymore, but this day still is, though it grows older with every passing minute. I'm imagining all sorts of political cache I could collect if I turned you over to your mother. Why, I might even get an actual, honest to goodness, face to face meeting with her."

"There's equally a chance that you'd end up dead," Vox said. "As the Queen isn't likely to believe that you weren't an accomplice of Nax."

Kel wagged his finger at Vox. "Yes, that's a very good point. Perhaps somebody here could enlighten me as to how I got entangled with your story before you arrived here?" He looked back and forth between Nax and Vox. When neither of them answered, he said, "No? Well, I guess it'll be another mystery for my diseased ridden mind to obsess over every night as I try to fall asleep."

"We need access to the Sicurezza Vault," Vox said.

Kel didn't say anything for a long moment. "As we have already established, it's generally agreed upon that I don't have the strongest grip on reality," Kel said. "So, you'll forgive me, but the last time I checked, this," he gestured to the room around them, "isn't the Vault."

"No, it's not," Vox agreed. "But I have it on good

authority that you've been trying to gain access to the vault for a few years."

"Good authority?" Kel echoed. "Whose authority exactly? The Queen? That doesn't sound like the sort of thing she'd go around sharing with people outside her inner circle." He glanced at Nax. "No offense."

"None taken," Nax replied.

"You're not denying it," Vox said.

"What's there to deny?" Kel held up his hands. "Name me a political figure on this planet who wouldn't want access to our people's most closely guarded secrets."

"You've taken it a step further than that," Vox said. "You've managed to get a data portal into the Vault."

"Even if I had done such a thing, it would be highly illegal," Kel said.

"I don't think you're particularly concerned with the legalities of things these days."

Kel glanced at Nax again. "No, I suppose not." Kel pressed his fingertips together. "Even if I had this theoretical data portal into the Vault, despite its questionable legal status, how would this be of interest to you?"

"We need access to it," Vox said.

"Yes, you mentioned that already," Kel said. "I'm looking for *specifics*." He fell silent for a moment. "There is a planet-wide manhunt on for the Royal Family's wayward son. It's rather remarkable you made it even this far without getting caught. Making your way to the Vault would be the equivalent of delivering yourself back into your mother's hands. What is in the Vault that you are so desperate for, that you would put yourself into this particular situation, I wonder?" When neither of them answered, Kel added, "That was not intended as a rhetorical question."

Nax wordlessly turned to Vox and Kel followed his gaze.

"That's information I'm not prepared to share with you," Vox replied.

"That's an interesting position to take in a negotiation such as this," Kel said.

"Are you going to help us?" Vox asked, trying, and failing, to keep the desperation out of his voice.

Kel held up his hands in a helpless gesture. "Help you? Even if this data portal existed and it was within my means, I would have no access to anything in the Vault as I don't have the security clearance necessary to access those files."

"No, but he does." Vox gestured at Nax.

"Ah." Kel nodded. "Things are finally beginning to make some semblance of sense." He folded his hands on the table and leaned forward again. He didn't speak for a long moment, staring quietly at the pitcher of yasha, his eyes taking on an almost vacant expression. Kel coughed and flicked his gaze past the pitcher at Nax and Vox. "You are both aware that should I allow you access to this hypothetical data portal I may or may not have, and should His Majesty's security clearances still be valid, I will take complete advantage of this opportunity that has been presented to me the moment you have concluded your business?"

Vox gritted his teeth. "It's crossed my mind."

"Of course it has," Kel said. He looked back and forth between them. "This is something that can never be undone. There are rumors, you know, of documents within the archives of the Vault that date back well over five hundred years. Meticulous records, I'm told."

"Our concerns are a little more recent," Vox said.

"Of course they are." Kel sat back. "Well, assuming we are all as real as we say we are and none of this is a figment of any of our potentially diseased minds, let's get on with it."

32

"HE SAW ME," Hawkins said. "At least, it *felt* like he saw me."

Nax didn't say anything.

"He couldn't have seen me, though. Right?"

Nax didn't respond.

"Because if he saw me," Hawkins continued. "Well, then, what does that mean? Am I real? Or am I somebody else's bizarre hallucination? If I'm in your mind, it's not possible for anyone else to see me. And yet, it sure felt like he saw me."

Nax closed his eyes for a second and took a deep breath.

"Is there a thing," she continued, "where people with Fey's can communicate on a different level than other people? Maybe through pheromones?" She shook her head. "No, that sounds stupid. It must have been something in your body language. A micro expression or something. That's really the only thing that makes sense. He picked up on that and then looked at where you were unconsciously directing some portion of your attention. That has to be it."

Nax exhaled slowly.

Hawkins leaned in and whispered in his ear. "If I'm

worried, then you should be worried and if you're not worried, then why am I worried?"

Nax opened his eyes and didn't say anything. He kept his gaze forward.

Hawkins took a step back. "Well, okay then."

33

KEL'S PEOPLE blindfolded the both of them.

"I hope you understand," Kel said. "I must take precautions."

Vox tried to protest, but he didn't try very hard.

Kel sat next to Nax in a vehicle that Nax couldn't identify, moving in a direction that he couldn't discern. The blindfold was absolute. He could see nothing. But he still heard everything.

In the darkness, Kel's breath sounded labored and strained.

He listened for some audible sign of Vox, uncertain if they were seated together and even more uncertain as to whether or not he even cared.

However, Nax instantly identified the sound of Hawkins' breathing to the left of him.

"Tell me, Your Majesty," Kel said after an indeterminable period of time. "Why did you leave?"

Nax didn't answer right away. Partly he was waiting to hear if Vox interrupted. Mostly he was waiting to hear if

Hawkins had anything to say first. When neither of them spoke, he said, "I'd rather you not call me that."

"No? I suppose you wouldn't. It must sound weird, after all these years, suddenly being addressed in such a manner," Kel said. "

"I wasn't very fond of it before, either," Nax said.

"No? I won't lie, that comes as a surprise," Kel said. "I can't imagine a single Natuzzi who wouldn't trade places with you." He paused and then added, "Well, obviously, not now, of course. But, *before*. I certainly would have."

Nax didn't say anything.

"Did they know? The people you served with on your ship? Did they know who you were?"

"Yes," Nax replied. "They knew who I was."

"Oh?" Kel sounded surprised. He fell silent for another moment. "Ah, I suspect you're playing a language game."

Nax didn't say anything.

"They knew who you were as a *person*, but not the fact that you were a member of a Royal Family?"

"It never came up," Nax answered.

"I imagine it wouldn't," Kel said. "What was it like? Living out there? In a life free from all of this?"

"Very fulfilling."

"That's good to hear."

Kel fell silent again. After what felt like a minute, he said, "You didn't answer my question."

"Why did I leave?"'

"I would imagine that you were living a charmed life here," Kel said. "At the very least, had you stayed, you would have never been charged with High Treason and faced with the death penalty."

Nax didn't answer.

He heard rustling as Kel nodded his head.

"Fair enough, I suppose," Kel said. "If you'll permit me this one question, though: Is it true?"

Nax felt Hawkins' hot breath in his ear. "Yes."

"And was it worth it?"

"Absolutely," Nax replied without hesitation.

"Then I suppose that's all that matters in the end."

"Is there something specific you're looking for?" Nax asked.

"Not particularly," Kel admitted. "But this is a unique opportunity and I didn't want it to go to waste. I've never spoken to anyone who's left our sector before."

"I did," Nax said.

"Oh?"

"Before I left," Nax said. "She lived in the village that I was...relegated to."

Nax heard Kel shift in his seat, moving in closer. "Fascinating. Who was she?"

"A poet," Nax replied.

"A poet? Not exactly the type of person one would imagine heading out among the stars," Kel said.

Nax paused before continuing. "She served aboard the *Veiled Patriot* as the Chief Medical Officer."

"The *Veiled Patriot*..." Kel trailed off as he searched his memories. The ship sounded familiar. It took a moment before he could recall the details. "Ah, yes. They were part of the Destorian Expedition." He paused. "Except, as I recall, all three vessels in that expedition were destroyed. There were no survivors."

Nax didn't respond.

After a moment, Kel rested a hand on Nax's shoulder. "Things become clearer, yes. Whether it's for the best or not, who can say."

There was a sound as the vehicle came to a stop.

"Ah," Kel announced. "We're here."

34

THE MACHINE WAS nothing like Nax had ever seen before. It looked like something that had been assembled by a blind man who had been working from a vague description of what a computer was supposed to be.

"It may not look like much," Kel said. "But no other has come this close."

Thick cables ran from the back of the console into ragged, hurriedly made holes in the concrete wall. The machine hummed as one of Kel's people powered it up and Nax felt the floor beneath his feet vibrate.

"Where are we?" Vox asked, looking around.

The cavern had an underground feel to it. The walls were damp with condensation. Pillars were spaced out every fifteen feet or so. There were no windows and the air was flat and stale. It had been years since Nax had even set foot on his home planet and his sense of direction hadn't been the same since the ghost of Hawkins had appeared, but he still recognized the ruins of Cascar.

"I'm not going to answer that question," Kel said, looking

around for a comfortable chair. He found one against a pillar and gestured for it to be brought over to the machine. "It's not something you need to know and, obviously, it's not something I feel comfortable sharing with you."

"How close are we to the Vault?" Vox asked. "You have to have a physical cable connection, right?"

"I'm not going to answer that, either," Kel said. "The agreement was that I allow you access to my resources, not that I explain to you how I came to having these resources."

Vox looked at Nax, maybe to see if he would provide an answer instead, or maybe he thought Nax had a suggestion for drawing out a more preferable answer from Kel. But Nax simply shrugged.

Frustrated, Vox turned to the machine. The screen flickered to life and the login portal to the Sicurezza Vault appeared. He started to approach it, but Kel made a noise that made him hesitate.

Vox watched impatiently as Kel sat down and rested his hands atop his cane. He cleared his throat. "I would assume that both of you understand the significance of what I have here? This is *unprecedented* in our people's history. The Sicurezza Vault is one of the most secure locations on Natuzzi. There is not a single console on this planet that can access it or attempt to access it without being immediately flagged. And here I have the one exception to the rule."

Nax stared at the login screen and then turned to Kel. "And yet, you still can't actually access anything."

"True. But I believe the effort itself is worth the credit. This is the sort of thing that simply isn't done. I think that we can all agree that the fact the Queen's gestapo haven't rushed down and killed us all is a miracle in its own right."

"A minor miracle," Nax said.

"But still a miracle, nonetheless," Kel said. "Do you

know how many individuals your mother has prosecuted in the last year for even speculating that such a thing was possible? Thirty. And that's down from the previous year, which was over a hundred. This device has sat here for nearly *three years undetected*."

"So you want credit for not doing anything and not getting caught for it?" Nax asked. He gestured to Vox who was growing more impatient by the second. "He knew about it."

"Which is very different from the Queen knowing about it," Kel said. "Obviously."

"Obviously," Nax echoed again. " He turned to look at Vox, but that was simply an excuse to look around the room without drawing any suspicion. Hawkins had disappeared. He couldn't decide if he felt abandoned or relieved.

"Are we waiting for anything else here?" Vox asked. "Another longwinded, conspiracy-riddled monologue?"

Kel sighed. "I just wanted to give this moment the respect it deserves. After all, we're about to commit one of the greatest crimes in the history of our people. The information that my organization will acquire from the Vault will change the very nature of our destiny."

"Momentous," Nax said. "I believe that's the word you're looking for."

Kel grinned at him. "Yes. *Momentous*." He coughed again. "I like that."

Nax took a deep breath. "And what's to stop my mother from simply killing all of you when it's done?"

"Nothing, of course," Kel said. "But it's almost impossible to kill an idea and once these ideas are released...Well, I don't believe your mother is prepared for the kind of uprising she'll be facing."

Nax looked at him, and raised his brow. "I don't think you know my mother as well as you think you do."

"I don't think you are wrong," Kel agreed.

"What exactly do you think you're going to find in the Vault?"

"Nothing less than what you found in that small village you were exiled to: the truth."

"The truth," Nax murmured.

"Tick-tock." Vox twirled an impatient finger. "We're running out of time here." He gestured to the screen on the machine. "It's your time to shine."

"Yes. My time to shine." Nax turned back to the machine.

"I'm sensing some hesitation on your part," Kel said. "Perhaps you're not comfortable with the cost of this endeavor?"

"No, I am not," Nax said. He stepped up to the screen and entered his credentials.

"Not comfortable with the cost, but in the end all too willing to pay the price," Kel said. "I will not lie: You surprise me."

The screen went blank and for a moment it seemed like nothing was going to happen.

Then the screen lit up again with full access to the entire Sicurezza Vault.

"Hell, yeah." Vox pushed back Nax and started searching through the records.

Nax took a step back, again glancing around for Hawkins and, again, not finding her.

"Looking for something?" Kel asked him quietly. "Some*one*, perhaps?"

Nax glanced at him out of the corner of his eyes. "Who would I be looking for?"

Kel shrugged. "I don't know. It's your hallucination, not mine. But she seems quite taken with you."

Nax's eyes widened with surprise, he started to say something, but Vox spoke first. He jerked his head around, expecting Vox to be listening in, but he wasn't. Vox's sole focus was on the machine's screen, a numb expression on his face.

"I don't believe it," he whispered.

"What is it?" Nax asked.

Vox didn't answer him. The color drained from his face.

Unwilling to move from his seat, Kel gestured for one of his people to approach the machine. After a moment of reading, he looked up at Kel. "It's something called *The Tyrant of Paradise*."

Kel frowned. "That has a ring of a distinctly non-Natuzzi nature about it."

"It's Veneer," Nax explained.

Kel looked mildly surprised. "Interesting."

"Vox," Nax started.

Vox stumbled back from the machine. He turned to Nax, a vacant look of horror on his face. "She's out of her damn mind."

"Who?" Nax asked.

"The Queen, obviously," Kel said. He leaned forward excitedly. "Don't keep us in suspense any longer. To what devil has she sold the soul of our people to?"

Vox looked at them, but his gaze wasn't focused on them. "Nearly half the Natuzzi fleet has been deployed out to the Veneer border." His voice sounded hollow. "According to this...they have orders to escort it out of Veneer space and into Natuzzi custody."

"What is it?" Nax asked.

"It's something purchased from the Oxean Syndicate," Vox said.

"This is getting more salacious by the moment," Kel said. "What could the Veneer have that the Queen would be willing to acquire through negotiations with one of the most despised, corrupt and deviant organizations in our galaxy?"

Vox finally was able to focus his gaze on them. "It's a planet killer."

35

THE WORDS DIDN'T MAKE any sense.

Planet killer.

Planet killer?

There was no context for the idea, the notion.

Neither Nax or Kel had the background or the imagination to fully understand the implications of what Vox had said because there existed no context for it.

Planets can't be killed. No one had the technology for that. They could be ravaged. They could be ruined. But killed? Utterly destroyed? That wasn't a thing that was possible.

Kel flexed his grip around the head of his cane. "Planet killer?" he repeated. "I'm afraid you're going to need to be a little more specific."

"I don't know how much more specific you want me to be," Vox snapped. Suddenly he was past his shock. "The Veneer built something that destroys actual planets and according to this," he gestured to the screen, "the Natuzzi are about to be in possession of it within the next twenty-six hours."

"I suspect there are some crucial details I'm missing here," Kel said. "Something that helps make this make sense. Why would the Veneer have created such a device?"

Nax moved closer to the machine to read the reports for himself. "These designs, these energy signatures, this is the Unity." He turned to Vox. "You knew."

Vox folded his arms and looked away. "Not specifically."

"Not specifically?" Nax repeated in frustrated disbelief.

Vox shot him a look. "Common sense says that any dealings with what's left of the Veneer Empire these days are going to have some involvement with them, one way or anything."

"Which means you knew," Nax repeated.

"I had suspicions," Vox said. "But I sure as hell didn't suspect *this*."

"What else?"

"What else?" Vox echoed.

"What else do you know that you're not telling me?" Nax asked.

"Plenty," Vox replied. "This is *my* mission, not yours."

"You pulled me into this," Nax said.

"That doesn't give you carte blanche over the whole damn thing."

"If this is the Unity-"

"Hey!" Vox snapped, glancing nervously around at Kel and his people. "Watch what you're saying."

Nax pointed at him. "You're the one who involved them."

Kel cleared his throat. "I hate to be the one left out of the conversation. So would one of you care to explain who or what this 'Unity' is?"

Vox clammed up.

Kel's brow went up. "Well, that is an interesting turn of events."

"The Unity is Species Four-Eight-Seven-Six," Nax said.

"Well," Kel replied in a breathy whisper. "I take it back. *That* is an interesting turn of events."

Vox glared at Nax, but Nax brushed him off with a dismissive wave. "Now is not the time."

"Now is *exactly* the time," Vox hissed at him.

"We don't know what my mother's intentions are for this device," Nax said.

"We can make some pretty educated guesses," Vox replied.

"And in the end, that's all they would be: *guesses*."

Vox frowned. "Why the hell are you suddenly defending her like this?"

"Because at the end of the day, regardless of anything and everything she has done, she is still his mother," Kel said. "The bonds of blood are the hardest to break." He pulled himself to his feet. "I would appreciate it if one of you would tell me what's going on here. What's *really* going on here. Because, despite my questionable hold on the nature of reality, even I can discern that not everything is as it seems in this moment."

Neither Vox nor Nax spoke up.

Kel nodded, as if expecting this reaction. He gestured to his people and several of them suddenly unholstered weapons and pointed them at Nax and Vox.

Vox glared at him. "This wasn't the agreement."

"No, you're right," Kel agreed. "The agreement was that I allow you access to my data portal into the Sicurezza Vault and I get to bear the fruits of His Majesty's access codes. However, it's become clear to me that the situation has either rapidly changed or was something more than you presented it to me as. Either way, I feel comfortable in saying that I have stayed true to our original agreement. I gave you access and I get to enjoy the fruits of said access. Now we find ourselves in something different. Something new. And I think that will necessitate a new agreement."

Kel took a few steps to the left, moving closer to the machine. "Let's begin with the fact that you are not who you say you are."

Vox looked at Nax.

Kel shook his head. "No, not him. *You*." Kel pointed at Vox. "You have always presented as something of an interesting mystery, Vox: a low-ranking official within the palace willing to risk his very life to simply build a line of communication with me and the Soldem Party? That's practically suicidal in our current political climate. And yet, you have managed to stay very much alive for far longer than I would have ever suspected. At first, I simply attributed this to luck on your part. Things have been, well, not exactly stable of late. And yes, I know that I am certainly to blame for some of that. But none of this happens in a vacuum, as it were.

"So then I began to entertain the thought that perhaps you were a double agent." Kel nodded. "This made the most sense. It sounded exactly like the sort of thing the Queen would engage in: dispatching a mole into the organization of one of her most volatile political opponents. And if we're being honest, this was an explanation I rather liked, because it provided me with an asset of the Queen to manipulate at my will."

Kel took a long pause, tapping his index finger against the head of his cane. "But of late, however, you have been displaying behaviors that are...Well, how best to put this?" Kel leveled his gaze at Vox. His eyes were sharp and focused. "You have been distinctly un-Natuzzi like."

It felt as though the temperature in the cavern dropped several degrees.

"That's because he's not Natuzzi."

Everyone turned at the new voice.

Queen Xie stood at the entrance of the Cascar cavern. Dozens of the royal guard spilled into the space.

There were shouts of confusion and surprise.

Kel's men moved to intercept, but it was too late.

The guardsmen had their weapons drawn and fired as they moved through the room.

Every one of Kel's people dropped dead before they even had a chance to return fire.

Nax had a brief second to acknowledge the look of horror on Vox's face before a single plasma bolt pierced his forehead, dissolving his head into a shower of gore and ashes.

Nax turned to Kel, but the old man had already been felled himself. He dropped to the ground, his final expression one of, 'Well, of course, this was going to happen.'

Within mere seconds of the Queen announcing her presence, the royal guards had successfully executed every single person.

Except for Nax.

There wasn't so much as a plasma burn on him.

The Queen took a deep breath and regarded her son, seemingly oblivious to the death and carnage that surrounded him. "Well, here we are again."

36

THE SOUL OF OBSESSION

"Ah. You're awake again."

Bendare lifted her head and tried to open her eyes. One was swollen shut and the other was so sensitive that the brilliant light of the room stung at her cornea and she immediately squeezed it shut again. She rolled her head to the side, hoping to block some of the light and slowly opened her eye again, this time no more than a crack.

The man with blond hair neatly parted to the side stood in front of her, holding that short, flat device, no longer than his hand and no thicker than an inch wide. It was a smaller version of what the other two had held when they had burst in before. What had he called it? He had called it something. He wanted her to know what it was, he had made that very clear. It was important to him that she understood what he was using to hurt her.

But all she could remember was the *pain*.

The pain was still with her now. Dulled somewhat, but still there, reminding her with every breath she took. Every part of her body where he had touched the torture device still stung painfully, as though she had been attacked by a group of Iarctec honey bees.

She was still tied to the chair. Bendare tried to turn her head slightly to see if Jacoby was in the room, but violent, stinging pain flared up in her neck and she stopped immediately.

"Yes," he said. "Moving is not a good idea. At least not until you've received medical attention. Which, if we're being honest, is not likely something you're going to be getting any time soon."

He grabbed an empty chair and sat down across from her. He exhaled a heavy sigh. "You are not what I expected at all."

Bendare didn't reply. She licked at her dry, cracked lips and tried to figure out where she was. She was clearly still on *The Soul of Obsession*, of that much she was certain. Beyond that, though, everything had a topsy-turvy, inside-out feeling to it. The walls were closing in on her and moving out at the same time. She swallowed. There was a strong possibility that she was suffering from an extreme concussion.

The man with the blond hair crossed his legs and let the torture device sit casually in his lap. "I read your file on the way here. It was remarkable. How much you've accomplished and how you've failed to suffer any legal complications for it. You would have been a valuable resource to bring into our fold."

Bendare blinked her one good eye and focused on him, confused.

He read the question on her face as easily as if she had spoken it. He shook his head. "Oh, no. This isn't a twisted sales pitch. No, I am afraid that particular ship has sailed,

Ms. Bendare. I'm not here to bring you into the fold. I'm here to deliver...*punitive measures.*"

She coughed up black blood.

He grimaced and carefully inched his chair back.

Bendare noticed this with some satisfaction and carefully worked her tongue around her abused mouth and then spat a thick wad of blood at him. It splattered against the floor just short of his feet.

He glanced down at the black stain and frowned. "Well, that certainly seems more in line with what I read about you."

"Kill you," Bendare said. Her voice was nothing more than a hoarse whisper.

"Yes, I'm sure you would, given the opportunity," he replied. "But it's an opportunity I do not intend to let you have." He leaned forward, resting his forearms on the back of his legs. "You involved yourself with something you had no business in."

Confusion was all over her face. He was visibly disappointed.

He settled back in his seat again and pointed the device at her. She flinched, but he didn't activate it. "The Church is aware of your role in the actions that were taken against Reverend Cavige." He let the statement hang there for a moment, waiting to see what kind of reaction there would be. Her one good eye focused on him as it clicked into place. "There we go. We're all on the same page now." He lowered the device back to his lap. "You provided...*interference*, I suppose would be the best way to describe it. Your legal team created a situation wherein we were otherwise encumbered when we should have been providing aid to Reverend Cavige. And because of that, Cavige is unjustly held against his will within a UPA jail where they will attempt to try him for crimes he did not commit." He took a deep breath and exhaled slowly. "Normally, you and your organization wouldn't be on our radar. We don't particularly care one way or another about your kind." He paused and then added, "I speak, of course, of your 'kind' as those who engage in criminal activities. I have nothing against your people, the Chirotians. I have met several Chirotians who I might have considered friends if circumstances were different."

"Criminal..." Bendare started to laugh, but it quickly turned into a painful cough.

He frowned again. "You seem to think there's no difference between what we have done here today and your... enterprising activities. But there is. You see, Ms. Bendare, this is *holy retribution* for your actions."

"The hell it is," she groaned.

"Absolutely," the blond-haired man agreed. "Absolutely." He pressed his hands together, cracking his knuckles. "Regardless, the point is that you've done something that we, in good conscience, cannot let go unaddressed. And so here I am, addressing it."

Bendare struggled to sit upright. "Where's Jacoby?"

A sour, distasteful expression passed across his face. "Your associate has been moved to another location," he replied. "He's proven to be...more difficult than we had prepared for."

Bendare grinned.

"That's not something to be proud of," he said. "We weren't dispatched here with orders to execute you and your associate." He held up a finger. "However, it's certainly within my authority to do so."

"What authority?"

He straightened up in his seat. "The authority bestowed upon me by the Church of Eternal Clarity. The same authority that took control of this vessel and has brought you and your organization to its knees."

Bendare struggled fruitlessly against her bonds.

"Please, you're just going to hurt yourself," he warned her. "And given the amount of pain you must already be under, I don't think you want to exacerbate it any further."

Bendare took a deep breath in an effort to steady herself. She focused on him as best she could with her one good eye. "I want you to listen to me very carefully."

"Are you going to beg for forgiveness?" he asked. "Confess your sins? I can't promise you anything, but it certainly wouldn't hurt your chances of survival."

There was a hissing noise as she exhaled slowly through her nose. "I am going to *kill* you," Bendare said. "I'm going to kill you, anyone you brought on this mission, your family, their families, your friends, their friends and anyone else who has ever heard of you. I'm going to kill you and then wipe you from the history books."

He sighed. "No, you're not." He got up and flicked on the device, pressing it against her collarbone.

Bendare screamed in pain as the energy jolted through her body. It felt as though every nerve ending was being shredded apart, pieced back together and then shredded apart again.

"Do you understand yet?" he asked her, raising his voice just enough so that she could hear him over her screaming. "No one is going to help you. To rescue you."

He pulled the device back from her and Bendare gasped in relief. She sucked in air desperately, hoping that it would stem the tide of pain, but it didn't.

"You can't..." she wheezed.

"I already have," he said, adjusting the setting on the device. "By this time tomorrow, there will be nothing left of the organization you built out of the humble beginnings of your father's business. Should I decide to let you live, you will be nothing less than a space pauper, without so much as a planetary citizenship to your name. In life or death you will have but one purpose, which is to be a lesson to anyone else who would consider moving against the Church of Eternal Clarity. Strike against us, even nothing more than a harmless swat, and we will destroy you *completely*."

Bendare bit her tongue in an attempt to pull her focus from the pain wracking her body. It worked and for a split second, she could almost think clearly again. "The Alliance-"

The blond-haired man laughed. It was a strange sound coming from him. It almost sounded disturbingly child-like. "Really?" he asked when he finally stopped laughing. "You think the UPA is going to help *you*?"

She glared at him. "I have resources."

"Not anymore you don't." He brushed some lint from his jacket. "And, for that matter, neither will the UPA. No, even if they were inclined to assist you, and they most assuredly are not, they're not going to be in much of a position to help. After I'm done with you, I'll be dealing with them."

Bendare just stared at him for a few moments. Eventually, she said, "Even I'm not crazy enough to think I can take on an interplanetary alliance and live to tell about it."

"Well that's the difference between you and us," he said. "We're not crazy."

Bendare flexed against her bonds.

"Now," he continued. "Let's talk about *you*. What do you think your punishment should be? Despite everything, I'm not leaning towards execution. Although, I'm not discounting it completely. It's less of a punishment and more of a final *solution*. And I don't think we need that.

We've taken everything away from you, yes. But that's more about a message to the galaxy at large. I think you personally need a form of punishment. Something...educational. Something that will broaden your horizons and help you become a better person. Something that will help you to remember not to stray into matters that aren't your concern." He tapped the torture device against his leg as he studied her. "You find a certain satisfaction in physical pursuits. According to the report I was given, you even derive some of your power from your physical body. So, perhaps," he raised the device and touched it to her breast. He didn't activate it, but Bendare flinched all the same. "Perhaps, then, you need to be scarred? Crippled? Maimed?"

Bendare's struggle against her bonds became more frantic.

"Please, stop," he said. "It's unbecoming."

"I'll kill you," Bendare hissed at him.

"Not if I do this correctly." He pulled the device back and adjusted the settings. A bolt of energy arced across its prongs, flickering for a moment before settling into a steady beam. "This is going to hurt quite a bit," he said. "Please take this opportunity to reflect on the mistakes that brought you to this moment."

37

"ABBOT WALLEN," the clergyman greeted the blond-haired man as he stepped back into what used to be Bendare's office.

Wallen set the torture device down on the desk. He pulled a cloth from his pocket and wiped the black blood from his hands. He closed his eyes for a moment, letting himself rest in the silence of the room. The echo of Bendare's screams faded a little faster with every passing second. He took a deep breath and opened his eyes.

"Everything went well?" the clergyman asked, glancing up at Wallen.

"As well as can be expected in a situation such as this," Wallen said. He noted the Vulderran bloodstains across the clergyman's outfit. "And you? A problem with the Vulderran?"

"Hm?" The clergyman looked confused for a moment. Wallen gestured to the stain and the clergyman looked down in mild surprise. "Ah. Yes. That. Well, yes. He was difficult, but in the end, we were still able to gain access to their records."

Wallen looked around the empty office. "Where is Bartram?"

"Attending to the crew," the clergyman answered. "Providing them with an opportunity for confession and conversion."

Wallen nodded approvingly. "He's a good man."

The clergyman turned back to the records in front of him. "Bartram never had the patience for paperwork."

Wallen grinned and clapped him on the shoulder. "And that's why I brought you. Have you found anything noteworthy?"

"Ms. Bendare has quite the extensive data archive," the clergyman replied "Several rather salacious reports on government officials within the UPA, as well as the Elwat, the Aurrod, and Phaw governments. I've flagged them all for your review at a later date."

"Good work," Wallen said. "I'm sure this will bear good fruit for the church."

"Yes, well, there was also this." The clergyman pulled up a report. "This is a recent report that Ms. Bendare commissioned from a contact within the Oxean Syndicate."

Wallen frowned distastefully.

"Yes, yes, I know," the clergyman agreed. "But, hear me out. According to this, the Natuzzi have been engaged in purchasing a device of sorts from the Syndicate."

Wallen sighed. "I don't see much merit in anything that may come from the Oxean Syndicate."

"It's a Veneer ship," the clergyman continued. "Called the *The Tyrant of Paradise*. According to this, it's considered a weapon of mass destruction."

Wallen paused and then leaned in over the clergyman's shoulder to look at the report himself. "Mass destruction?"

"More specifically?"

"Are there more specifics?" Wallen asked.

The clergyman looked up at him from the tops of his eyes. "They call it a planet killer, sir."

"A planet killer," Wallen repeated. "That is an interesting turn of phrase."

"According to this, I don't believe it's just a turn of phrase," the clergyman said. "It was something the Veneer developed with the aid of a species referred to as the Unity."

"I'm not familiar with them."

"Reading between the lines, I believe the Unity may be Species Four-Eight-Seven-Six."

Wallen took a sharp, deep breath.

The clergyman nodded. "According to this report that Ms. Bendare acquired, the Natuzzi will be taking custody of the *The Tyrant of Paradise* within the next twenty-six hours," the clergyman said. "The report mentions a potential window of opportunity to disrupt that delivery."

Wallen continued to read over the clergyman's shoulder. "Is there something specific on your mind?"

"As I understand it, the Church leadership is struggling with a proportional response to the Alliance in response to Reverend Cavige's arrest," the clergyman said.

"It's a topic of conversation, yes," Wallen admitted.

"If I may be so bold, Abbot," the clergyman said, gesturing to the diagram of the Veneer vessel. "This may provide us with a response that would be appropriately proportional."

Wallen studied the diagram of the *The Tyrant of Paradise* as it slowly rotated. After a long moment, he nodded. "Yes, I think you may be on to something."

38

NATUZZI

"WELL." Queen Xie looked around the cavern, apparently oblivious to the death and carnage that surrounded her son. "I have not been down here in forever." Her gaze settled on the machine. "Clearly that was a mistake."

The royal guardsmen moved quickly, efficiently and quietly, clearing a path through the bodies and blood for the Queen. She walked without looking and approached her son. She cupped the side of his face in a loving gesture.

"Thank you," she said.

Nax struggled to remain composed. The stench of death slowly filled the air. Everything had happened so quickly, he was still trying to process it. His mother, the Queen, was *here*. Vox was dead. Kel was dead. And...

Nax felt his mind trail off into nothingness and his gaze drift down to Vox's headless corpse. The blood that splattered around the body was a deep red, a sharp contrast to the teal blood of the Natuzzi bodies.

He looked at his mother.

"Well, I wouldn't be much of a world leader if I didn't know when there was a spy in my midst." The Queen took a step back. One of the guardsmen grabbed the chair Kel had been using and moved it around for her. She settled into it, crossing her legs and resting her hands on her knees. Despite the scene of bloody carnage, she looked as regal and royal as she did when presiding in the throne room.

Nax felt his legs finally give out. He started to fall back and was surprised to find there was another chair waiting for him. He looked up to find a guardsman standing just behind him, looking almost apologetic.

"You're still a member of the Royal Family, despite your questionable actions," the Queen said. "And you will continue to be treated as such until I say otherwise. Don't be so surprised."

Nax rubbed a hand across his tired face. He still didn't say anything. His mind was racing to catch up to the events that were unfolding around him.

Four guardsmen positioned themselves on either side of Nax and the Queen. Their plasma rifles still in hand, but pointed towards the floor. The rest of the unit begun the process of removing the bodies of Kel's men.

Nax sat back in his seat, eyeing the machine and then moving his gaze back to his mother.

"Yes?" she asked.

Nax didn't say anything. He just stared wordlessly at his mother.

The Queen nodded and looked around the empty space of the Cascar Cavern. "The last time I was down here you were six. You had something of an unhealthy obsession with these haunted landmarks. One hundred and twenty members of the Cascar Cavalry sacrificed their lives in this very spot, spilling blood that ended a nearly fifty-year war." She returned her gaze to him. "You said you thought it was brave. I never understood that, even to this day. Can you imagine the kind of world we would be living in if those one hundred and twenty souls hadn't committed suicide?"

"Probably one wracked with endless war," Nax replied in a whisper.

She shook her head. "You still don't understand. Sacrifices like that mean *nothing* if they're coming from the wrong side."

Nax looked at her, puzzled. "Wrong side?"

"The Natuzzi must always be in the right," she replied. "And the leadership of our people must always be seen as right."

"Even when it's wrong?"

She fixed him with a cold stare. "We are never wrong."

One of the guardsmen approached the Queen. He held a datapad with a fresh report. He said quietly, "We've taken the Tai cell."

She nodded. "Good. Thank you."

The guardsman stepped back.

"The Tai cell?" Nax repeated. "Cavon Tai."

The Queen nodded. "Yes. I had been hoping that Vox would eventually lead us to them, but he was far more cautious than I gave him credit for. Patience is a rare trait, one that I have had to work to develop and continue to struggle with every day against an administration that wants me to lash out immediately at every slight. Fortunately, my patience paid off and Vox was presented with a situation where he would inevitably throw caution to the wind. From that moment on, it was simply a matter of following from a distance and picking off the pieces as he went."

Understanding finally dawned on him. "You *used* me."

"Would you prefer that I had executed you the moment you stepped foot back on this planet?" she asked him. "Because that's what my advisers wanted me to do."

Nax looked around at the dead bodies that were rapidly disappearing. "Yes."

She sighed. "You're such a petulant child."

"And you're a blood-thirsty despot," Nax replied.

The four guardsmen flanking them abruptly lifted their rifles and aimed them at Nax.

Nax didn't flinch.

The Queen sighed and raised a hand. The guardsmen lowered their weapons.

"You would do well to take a moment and *think* before you speak, my son," she said. "Not everyone is as patient with you as I am." She smoothed out the creases in her white jumpsuit. "Yes. I used you. That is my prerogative as your Queen and your mother. More than that, though, it's my *responsibility*. That's something you've never seemed to understand: responsibility."

Nax gestured to the headless corpse of Vox and Kel's dead body. "Responsibility."

"I don't need your approval," she said.

"What did you do to Pastor Tai?" Nax asked, afraid that he already knew the answer.

"My men were given orders to execute on sight," she replied without hesitation.

"They were unarmed civilians," Nax said, horrified.

She raised a corrective finger. "They were terrorists intent on inciting rebellion and social unrest."

"And the appropriate response to that was to *kill them*?"

She looked at him with hardened eyes. "Do you not understand?"

"Apparently, I don't."

"We are at *war*."

Nax jerked back as if she yelled at him. He didn't say anything for a moment, trying to process the words.

"War?" Nax repeated. "War? Who are we at war with?"

"Everyone who is not Natuzzi," the Queen replied evenly.

He stared at her with abject horror. "You are out of your mind."

"Careful." She wagged a finger at him. "Dalin Kel said the same thing and look where that got him."

With all the bodies gone, save for Vox and Kel's, the guardsmen went to work on carefully dismantling the machine.

"In the last few hours you have had the unique experience of being able to see how fractured our planet is," the Queen said. "We're already under attack, from within," she gestured to Kel's corpse, "and without." She pointed to Vox's headless body. "I am trying to hold our people together with nothing less than the sheer force of my will and it is *tiring*."

The Queen closed her eyes and dropped her face into her hands. "Do you have any idea what it's like to be attacked every day by a new group of people? To be constantly told that everything you do is wrong? To be second-guessed on every decision?" She lowered her hands and looked up at him. "It is too much."

"So this is your solution?" Nax asked. "Kill anyone who doesn't agree with you?"

She scowled at him. "I should smack you for your insolence."

"It would make for a nice change of pace," Nax replied dryly.

The Queen got to her feet and kicked at Vox's corpse. "This human was an agent of the Alliance's Directive Fifty-Two. He was a *spy*, sent here to destabilize not just my administration, but our *people*. This was part of a calculated plan on behalf of the Alliance to manipulate us into being dependent on the UPA and as a result, open our borders and resources to the Alliance. We are a trusted and respected member of the Alliance and this is how they treat us? This was an open act of aggression and a declaration of *war*."

"That is a...liberal interpretation of a series of events that are, at best, convoluted," Nax replied.

"And it is my job as the leader of our people to simplify matters," she said. She pointed to Kel's corpse. "Dalin Kel has been leading an open insurrection on our very planet for over twenty years. He was also behind several covert attempts to overthrow my government and destabilize and decentralize the newsfeeds."

"Allowing the general public to make up their own minds about what's going on on our planet," Nax said.

The Queen scowled at him. "And finally, Cavon Tai was a heretic, spreading blasphemy and brainwashing our people with a false religion."

"It has been my experience that freedom of religion is considered to be a valuable right," Nax said.

"These are declarations of war, open acts of rebellion." The Queen glared at him. "How would you have me deal with them?"

Nax struggled to maintain his composure. "I can't say that I would have immediately jumped to execution without any kind of trial."

"Guilt was predetermined the moment they made their choice."

"Then you clearly had no choice," Nax replied flatly.

She looked at him for a long, hard moment. "I thought that, perhaps, during this...*endeavor*, you might finally come to an understanding."

"I did," Nax replied. "Unfortunately I don't believe it's the one you wanted."

The Queen shook her head sadly. She clasped her hands behind her back and walked over to what was left of the machine.

"My people had the hardest time trying to figure out where Kel was hiding this. I never would have imagined he put it in my own backyard," she said. "We knew he had built it and we knew he was attempting to gain access, but we couldn't complete a successful trace on it." She glanced back at Kel's corpse almost remorsefully. "I wish I could have asked him about it beforehand."

"We all have regrets," Nax replied.

The Queen sighed. "Yes, we do."

"I regret not going with my first choice all those years ago," Nax said. "Before deciding to leave."

"Oh?" She looked back at him. "And what was that choice?"

"Killing you."

The Queen's face hardened again. "I want you to know that, despite everything, I'm not going to have you executed."

Nax got up from his seat. "Am I supposed to be grateful?"

She shrugged. "Probably not, considering that you're going to live out the remainder of your life in a dark hole, cut off from the rest of civilization."

"But you're not bitter."

"No," she said. "But I'm *just*."

"What are you going to do with the Veneer planet killer?" Nax asked.

The Queen didn't answer him at first. She watched as her guardsmen removed the last of the machine. Slowly she turned back around to face her son. "I'm going to do whatever I must to protect my people and ensure there is no threat to our inherent destiny as masters of this universe."

"There was a time I would have agreed with you," Nax said. "But I've come to realize that we are masters of nothing. We are not the be all, end all of this universe."

She pointed at him. "And that's why I'm going to drop you down a dark hole."

"You don't know what you're dealing with," Nax said.

"I know exactly what I have," she replied. "Your Directive Fifty-Two is not the only one who can successfully plant a spy. I know all about the Unity and their collaboration with the Veneer Empire."

"Then you know that anything from the Unity is a poisoned chalice," Nax said.

"For anyone other than the Natuzzi, yes," she said. "But we are not the Veneer. We are *superior* to them."

"The Veneer are all but extinct because they made bedfellows with the Unity."

The Queen held out her hands, palms up. "As I said, we are superior."

"Only in the sense that we're not dead yet," Nax said.

The Queen gestured to the guardsman and they took custody of Nax. He didn't struggle in their grip.

"In less than twenty-six hours we will have *The Tyrant of Paradise* and this universe will learn not to threaten the Natuzzi," the Queen said.

"Can you really condemn an entire planet?" Nax asked.

A small, remorseful smile tugged at the corners of her lips. "I already have."

39

USS DEFIANCE

Somebody cleared their throat just behind Cooper. He swiveled in the command chair to find an old man with very bushy eyebrows standing just over his shoulder.

Cooper's gaze flicked to the rank and insignia on the badge. He recognized it immediately. "Can I help you, Doctor?"

Rabkin held out his hand. "Thought I should introduce myself."

Cooper turned back to the viewscreen, ignoring Rabkin's hand. "I am aware of who you are. I've read your file."

Rabkin's brow furrowed in disapproval. "I've read your file, too. Doesn't mean we shouldn't have ourselves a proper sit-down. Considering you went out of your way to talk to almost every member of Mitchell's senior staff, save for me."

"You're Mitchell's oldest friend," Cooper said. "I don't think you would be able to give an objective opinion on him."

"Is that what you're doing?" Rabkin asked. "You're trying to figure out what the objective truth of Gavin Mitchell is?"

"I'm just trying to get caught up," Cooper replied evenly. "I got dumped into the middle of something here."

"Every new XO gets dumped into the middle of something," Rabkin said. "Comes with the territory."

Cooper swiveled his chair back around to meet Rabkin's gaze. "I'm sorry. Did I give you the impression I asked for your advice on how to do my job?"

"Well, not directly, of course," Rabkin said. "But your actions certainly said it."

"You and I don't and won't have the same kind of relationship as you and Captain Mitchell," Cooper said.

"I should sure as hell hope not," Rabkin said. "That man is one of the most stubborn asshole commanders in the Fleet."

Cooper pressed his lips together tightly. "You seem to be having difficulty taking a hint, Doctor."

"Not at all," Rabkin replied. "I can absolutely tell when somebody's trying to tell me to fuck off without them actually saying it. I just don't give a damn."

Cooper closed his eyes and sighed. "What specifically did you feel you needed to say to me, Doctor?"

"Just wanted to advise you not to be an asshole," Rabkin said. "That job's already split between me and Mitchell. This ship doesn't need another one."

Cooper looked up at him, confused. "What is that supposed to mean?"

"It means that whatever Admiralty's reasons for sending you here, maybe you should actually take a moment and soak it all in before making any rash decisions."

Cooper just shook his head, a ghost of a smile on his face. "I'll keep that in mind, Doctor."

"You do that."

Cooper got to his feet and made his way over to Sadler's station. "What are you working on?"

Sadler looked up, startled.

He raised an eyebrow. "Is it something you shouldn't be working on?"

"No. You just startled me." Sadler turned back to the console. "The Natuzzi keep their newsfeeds closed off from the UPA. They don't export anything. No products, no media, no literature. *Nothing*."

"So they don't like sharing." Cooper rested a hand on the back of her seat. "Personally, I'm not fond of the concept either."

She glanced back at him. "You don't like to share? What are you, a six-year-old only child?"

"As a matter of fact I'm the oldest of six siblings," Cooper replied. "So when I say I have an aversion to sharing it's because I grew up having nothing of my own." He nodded at the screen. "So what are you working on?"

"Well, I figure, we're pretty close to the Natuzzi border," Sadler said. Her voice had a cautious tone. "We don't know what's going on with Nax. Nobody's telling us anything."

"They don't have to."

"I guess. That doesn't mean they have to be assholes about it."

"They're not being assholes, Ms. Sadler," Cooper said. "They just do things differently than we do. That doesn't make them assholes. It just makes them different."

"Well in my book and in this particular situation, it makes them different assholes."

He pointed to something on the screen. "This looks like you're trying to hack into their data signals."

"Well, that's because that's exactly what I'm doing."

Cooper frowned. "That's illegal."

"Technically, yes," Sadler said.

"There's nothing technical about it," he said. "Protocol is very clear on this matter. We have no legal standing to invade their privacy."

"Okay, well, before you court martial me, I want to point out that the way I'm doing it, the whole thing is a little grayer."

"Gray?" Cooper echoed, unconvinced.

"This close to their border, it's less hacking into something and more looking for a stray signal that happens to be transmitted out past their firewalls," Sadler said.

"That doesn't sound very gray to me," Cooper said.

"Maybe that's because you're being a little too black and white about this." Sadler took a moment to compose herself. "Look, I understand that Lieutenant Commander Nax is nobody to you, but to the rest us of he's a valued member of this crew. We deserve the right to know what's happening to him."

"Actually, you don't," Cooper said. "His fate is in the hands of the Natuzzi government and they don't owe this crew anything."

Sadler glared at him. "That's pretty cold."

"It's simply the facts. Do I have to order you to discontinue this course of action?"

Sadler didn't respond.

Cooper sighed. "I'm getting tired of saying this, but I'm not here to make new enemies."

"It certainly doesn't sound like you're interested in making new friends, either."

"There's nothing you'll be able to do about what is or isn't happening to Nax," Cooper said. His voice softened a little. "You're just opening yourself up to inevitable heartache. Trust me, you don't want to have a front seat when your friend is on death row."

"And if my friend is on death row, I wouldn't want him there alone," she replied.

Cooper shook his head. "You're simply going to be causing yourself unnecessary pain and when that happens, will I be able to count on you to follow through on your duties?"

"Are you asking if the crew is going to have an emotional breakdown if we happen to see Nax executed live?"

"No, I'm asking if *you* are going to have an emotional breakdown," Cooper said. "Because I don't have the time to stress out about the rest of the crew right now."

Sadler turned back to her console. "Hopefully that's not something we're going to have to worry about."

"That's not an answer."

"Sure it is," she said, finishing up. "It's just not one you want to hear because it makes it difficult for you to decide whether or not you want to throw me in the brig."

"I'm not going to throw you in the brig," he muttered. "Why does everybody always think I'm going to throw them in the brig?"

"Commander, incoming transmission from the Natuzzi newsfeeds," the ensign at the comm station announced.

Cooper looked at Sadler. She held up her hands.

"Not me," Sadler said. "If it was me, there wouldn't be an announcement about it."

"It's being pushed out over all the major feeds," the ensign added.

Cooper gestured to the viewscreen. "Put it up on the screen, ensign."

The track of Ahines' comet disappeared and was

replaced with the logo of the Natuzzi government presented against a white background.

After a few seconds of this, Cooper turned to the communications officer. "Ensign, are we missing something?"

The ensign double checked her console. "No, sir. Everything is-"

The logo abruptly disappeared and was replaced with a female Natuzzi dressed in a regal, all white outfit, sitting on a throne.

"To the members of the United Planetary Alliance, unaffiliated planets and the galaxy at large, I am Queen Xie of the Natuzzi people. This is an unprecedented event in our people's history. This is a real-time transmission that is being broadcast as widely as possible and in as many different languages as possible. No such broadcast has ever been sent from Natuzzi like this before and it is unlikely one will ever be sent like this again. Unfortunately, this is not a moment to celebrate.

"As many of you are already aware, we have been faithful, steadfast members of the United Planetary Alliance for hundreds of years. We believed that despite our faith, we would be able to maintain a relationship with our interstellar neighbors. We believed that it was possible to maintain a sense of harmony amidst a galaxy of discord.

"We were wrong."

A new image appeared next to the Queen. This one was of a human male in a Fleet uniform, slowly morphing into a Natuzzi male.

"Recently it came to our attention that the Alliance Admiralty authorized the placement of an undercover operative on our native soil." Queen Xie folded her hands together and leaned forward on her throne. "We did not ask for much. Simply that our beliefs and wishes were to be respected. They were not. Our home is *sacred*. Our people are *sacred*. To place an undercover operative of this nature, regardless of intent, is of the highest offense. We have asked for *nothing* from the Alliance. We have demanded *nothing*. All we asked for was that you leave us alone. And you could not even do that."

Queen Xie paused. Her body was trembling with rage. With every passing word her volume rose. Every sentence ended with a bitter, sharp snap, as if she was mere moments away from screaming at the galaxy. So she took a moment to compose herself.

When she began again, her voice had returned to a more normal volume.

"An act such as this would be considered one of war by any other administration. That is not who I am, nor is it who I wish to be. War benefits no one, least of all my people.

"But these actions cannot go unaddressed.

"Accompanied with this transmission, in addition to proof of our claims that an Alliance operative was found among our people, I am including coordinates for a small Alliance research colony on Vuna N-Seven. Legally speaking, this planet resides in a section of space that intersects with our border, the Veneer Empire and the Neutral Zone. Out of mutual respect, neither we nor the Veneer Empire have attempted to lay claim to Vuna N-Seven and have quietly allowed the UPA to maintain its research colony. That is no longer the case."

Queen Xie disappeared from the screen.

The transmission switched to live feed of Vuna N-Seven. There was a globe-shaped vessel in orbit around the planet. It was hard to determine its size, but in relation to the planet, it seemed to be no larger than the *Defiance*. It appeared to be built out of a strange, black material with an undulating appearance. Two rings encircled the vessel at opposing angles, spinning at almost a leisurely pace.

Queen Xie continued in voice over. "Vuna N-Seven is a Class M planet. Small by most standards. It has two moons and a few million indigenous lifeforms, although none of them classify as intelligent species. The only creatures on this planet that can think for themselves, reason, rationalize or communicate complex emotions, feelings, thoughts or facts are the three hundred members of the UPA Science Corps.

"This is not an act of war. This is a response. It is a warning. It is a promise. You have mistakenly thought us weak. We are anything but. The Natuzzi will not suffer at the hands of anyone. We will not be played for fools."

The spinning rings slowly detached from the vessel, separating into thousands of tentacles that seemed to pierce the planet.

There was a startled gasp from the ensign at the comm station as the tentacles slowly wrapped themselves around the planet and squeezed.

There was no sound over the next twenty minutes as Vuna N-Seven was slowly destroyed. No sound other than the soft sobbing of the various bridge crew members who were unable to properly comprehend what they were seeing.

By the end, Vuna N-Seven was gone and the vessel had grown approximately ten percent.

The screen switched back to Queen Xie.

It felt as if she made eye contact with every member of the bridge crew.

"This is your only warning," she said.

And then the screen went blank.

40

NATUZZI SCOUT SHIP

"We have to do something," Keane said after a minute. "We have to contact somebody. Wanamaker? This is..." He looked back at his captain. "I don't know what this is."

"Neither do I," Mitchell said grimly.

Keane looked over the controls almost helplessly. "Do we still go after Nax?"

"They're waiting for us," Mitchell said.

"You can't be certain."

"If they discovered Wanamaker's agent, I'm one hundred percent certain." Mitchell tapped him on the shoulder. "We need to get back to the *Defiance*."

"And then what?"

"We'll worry about that when we get back," Mitchell said.

"And what about Nax?"

Mitchell set his jaw. "I don't like it any more than you do. But this changes things and they sure as hell aren't changed for the better."

The proximity alarms suddenly went off and three

Natuzzi warships dropped out of hyperspace, surrounding them.

"Shit!" Keane exclaimed. He started evasive maneuvers.

The first Natuzzi vessel opened fire and took out their engines.

Mitchell raised his hands to cover his face as his console exploded.

Artificial gravity went out and the two men felt their bodies suddenly straining against the seat restraints as their ship tumbled through space.

A new transmission broke through the various alarms that were blasting throughout the small vessel.

"Alliance officers, you are in violation of Natuzzi law. Prepare to be taken into custody."

The ship shook with the telltale sign of a tractor beam taking hold.

"Shit," Keane said again. He looked back at his captain.

Mitchell wiped blood from an open cut on his cheek as he stared grimly out at the Natuzzi warship they were being pulled towards.

"Yeah," Mitchell agreed. "Shit."

41

NATUZZI

NAX LOOKED around his small cell that. It looked like a prison, but for some strange reason, it didn't necessarily feel like one.

There were two cots, a sink and a waste receptacle. There was no window. The only source of light came from a single bulb located out of reach above the door.

His mother stood in the doorway.

"I don't think I'll see you again," she said.

He stood with his back to her, unable to face her.

"I suspect you'll die down here," she continued. "It's possible that I may change my mind at some point in the future and consider clemency. But..." She paused and sighed. "I think we both know that's not going to happen."

Nax stared at the tiny cot. It was barely big enough to accommodate him. On the second cot, there was a large clump of bedding.

"I have left instructions with your sister," she continued. "Should something happen to me, I leave your fate in her hands. I will do my best to ensure that she treats your case with the objectivity it deserves. I want her to make any decisions based on facts and not out of some ill-conceived notion to follow through on what my wishes might be."

Nax tested the sink. A trickle of water came out.

Her voice softened. "This is not what I wanted for you. This is not how I imagined things would end between us. When I discovered you had left I was heartbroken and then to discover what you had been up to out there nearly destroyed me. No mother wants their child to end up like this. We all want the best for our offspring. And that's all I wanted for you. But what you did with that female was unforgivable."

Nax didn't say anything. He stared at the blank spot on the concrete wall.

"If there had been a child, I wouldn't even be granting you this," she said. "I would have executed you myself."

Nax didn't respond.

"I want you to know, that despite everything, I still love you, my son."

She stood there for another minute, staring at his back, waiting to see if he would turn to face her one last time.

He didn't.

The Queen nodded and stepped back out of the doorway.

A moment later, the door slammed shut.

Nax looked around the empty cell, wondering if Hawkins would appear. She didn't.

He sat down on the cot.

He knew he should be thinking about escape. He needed to get word to Wanamaker and Captain Mitchell. His mother needed to be stopped.

But instead, he found himself thinking about Dalin Kel and wondering how strong his own grip on reality was.

Because if this wasn't a prison, then what was it?

There was a sound from the other cot.

Nax looked up.

The lump of bedding moved and a figure sat up.

She was a Natuzzi female, dressed in threadbare rags. Her face was gaunt and her body was sinewy.

"I wasn't aware I was going to have a roommate," Nax said.

The Natuzzi woman didn't respond. She lifted her left hand from beneath the bedding. It held a blade that glinted in the dim light of the cell.

Nax looked at the blade and then into the eyes of the woman.

"Are you real?" he asked.

Her eyes burned with anger and hate.

"Yes," she said and got to her feet.

Nax didn't move from the cot, still not entirely certain. He looked at the blade, trying to wrap his mind around the idea of what this was.

"Who are you?" Nax asked.

"A willing vessel," she replied.

"For what?"

Instead of answering, she moved across the small cell with a graceful speed and slipped the knife into Nax's chest.

A small gasp of surprise escaped him.

He stared down at the blade's handle jutting from his chest, feeling the pain of the sharp metal tearing him apart. He felt his hand reaching up for the blade, as if needing to touch it to confirm that it was real. But then suddenly she yanked it out of his chest.

Nax jolted forward with the motion and toppled to the floor of the cell. Thick teal blood began pouring out of his chest.

She knelt over him, plunging the blade back into his chest, whispering, "Heretic."

The blade was yanked out again. More blood.

"Deceiver," she hissed, stabbing him again.

His body jolted as she yanked the blade out from between his ribs.

The floor of the cell was slick with his blood.

She leaned in close to his ear and whispered, "*Infidel,*" as she plunged the blade into his chest one final time.

Nax coughed up blood as his vision grew dim.

He couldn't feel any more pain, just an overwhelming numbness.

Everything slowly went dark.

And he wondered still, *is this real?*

42

USS DEFIANCE

ENSIGN EMILY WESTIN watched the transmission from Natuzzi in the privacy of her quarters. She chewed nervously on her thumbnail as she watched *The Tyrant of Paradise* destroy Vuna N-Seven. This was the third time she had watched it.

It was horrific. She was going to have nightmares for the rest of her life after watching the transmission.

And yet, she couldn't stop watching it.

As it came to the end, she restarted it, skipping through Queen Xie's opening monologue and muting the rest of it.

All she wanted to see was *The Tyrant of Paradise*.

This time she watched in slow motion. She leaned forward, her eyes only inches from the screen, as if she could discern some extra detail she had missed before.

Westin was unaware of it, but she had been crying for the last five minutes.

It was a natural reaction to viewing such a horrific event. But, somehow, she was numb to even that.

An alert appeared in the corner of the screen, informing her that she was on duty in twenty minutes.

Warrick had assigned her to clean out the thermal core chambers.

She swiped the alert away. Simple engineering tasks seemed unimportant now.

Another alert popped up on her screen. She nearly swiped this one away, too, before realizing it was a message.

It took a second to recognize the sender ID. When she did, she paused the transmission and opened the message immediately.

It read:

Sister Westin,

We hope this finds you well.

As you already have undoubtedly learned, the Natuzzi people have engaged a new weapon of mass destruction.

Attached to the message is detailed information on this weapon, its current location and its path of travel for the next twenty-six hours.

It is the decision of the Elders that a weapon of this nature should not be entrusted to the masses. Actions must be taken, and for the safety of the galaxy, we must take custody of this weapon.

You are currently the closest member of our flock. Please acknowledge receipt of this message and standby for further instructions.

Sincerely,
  Abbot Wallen

The Church of Eternal Clarity

Westin read the message twice.

She clicked over and watched the transmission once more, this time at normal speed.

The tentacles extended from *The Tyrant of Paradise* and pierced the planet below. A cold shiver ran down her spine. She finally became aware of her tears.

Westin wiped her eyes dry and immediately sent an acknowledgment of receipt and assured Abbot Wallen that she would be waiting for further instructions.

43

LASTLY, at approximately the same time as *The Tyrant of Paradise* began to destroy Vuna N-Seven, it transmitted a signal.

It was an undetectable signal and there was no real distance that would have kept it from reaching its source. It made its way across space effortlessly and completely unnoticed.

And in the patient room on the *USS Defiance*, the signal reached its source.

Ensign Erin Calloway woke up.

TO BE CONCLUDED IN:
THE VALUE OF TERROR

Subscribe to my newsletter and I'll let you know as soon as the next Defiance book is ready to read.

<u>Sign Up Here</u>

https://onestrayword.beehiiv.com/subscribe

Word-of-mouth is crucial for any author to succeed. If you enjoyed this book, please consider leaving a review, even if it's only a line or two. It would make all the difference and would be very much appreciated.

ABOUT THE AUTHOR

Jason Krumbine loves to write! He's happily married and lives in Orlando, FL where he enjoys visiting Disney World with his daughter and wife.

If you want to get an automatic email when Jason's next book is released sign up here:

https://onestrayword.beehiiv.com/subscribe

Your email address will never be shared and you can unsubscribe at any time.

ALSO BY JASON KRUMBINE

———————